MW00532925

DEAD MAN IN THE ORCHESTRA PIT

Other books by Tom Osborne

FICTION

Foozlers (a novel)
Tenth Avenue Bike Race
The Reamer's Car Club Blues Band Story

POETRY

Under the Shadow of Thy Wings
9 Love Poems
Please Wait for Attendant to Open Gate

DEAD MAN IN THE ORCHESTRA PIT

a novel

by TOM OSBORNE

ANVIL PRESS | VANCOUVER | 2006

Dead Man in the Orchestra Pit
Copyright © 2006 by Tom Osborne

All rights reserved. No part of this book may be reproduced by any means without the prior written permission of the publisher, with the exception of brief passages in reviews. Any request for photocopying or other reprographic copying of any part of this book must be directed in writing to ACCESS: The Canadian Copyright Licensing Agency, One Yonge Street, Suite 800, Toronto, Ontario, Canada, M5E 1E5.

LIBRARY AND ARCHIVES CANADA CATALOGUING IN PUBLICATION

Osborne, Tom, 1949-

    Dead man in the orchestra pit / Tom Osborne.

ISBN 1-895636-72-8

    I. Title.

PS8579.S36D42 2006   C813'.54   C2006-901390-X

Printed and bound in Canada
Cover design: Mutasis Creative
Cover & interior illustration: JT Osborne
Interior design & typesetting: HeimatHouse

Represented in Canada by the Literary Press Group
Distributed by the University of Toronto Press

The publisher gratefully acknowledges the financial assistance of the B.C. Arts Council, the Canada Council for the Arts, and the Government of Canada through the Book Publishing Industry Development Program (BPIDP) for their support of our publishing program.

Anvil Press Inc.
P.O. Box 3008, Main Post Office
Vancouver, B.C. V6B 3X5 CANADA
www.anvilpress.com

When Calliope's flight has failed thee
And Melpomene's the friend you've known,
Best don't think of lost ball games
And all the third-down calls you've blown."

—GRAFFITI, LOCKER ROOM WALL OF

THE CALGARY STAMPEDERS

"That 'Mad Joe' is quite the frigging buffoon nonpareil,
Mr. Dwyer."

—DUSTY MOONS, THE FIRST BLACK MAYOR

OF VANCOUVER

FOR SCOTT SITES
1954–2005
who relished in the pathos

Prologue

THE FAT MAN STRUGGLES to his feet saying, "No, no!" The cast rehearsing on stage freezes. The Fat Man, with hands braced on the seats in front of him for balance, assumes a trundling side-step left, making his way along the row to the aisle. Those sitting in the same row between him and the aisle climb over their seats to the row behind to let him by, the eyes of the Fat Man appearing as dark holes in fleshy pouches fixed upon the people on stage as he grunts and squeezes his bulk to the theatre aisle. Then he lumbers down to the front stage steps, large dark Hush Puppies flopping loudly on the carpet. The cast watches his approach while the orchestra, silent and unseen, sits motionless somewhere in the glow of the orchestra pit. The director, who is 51 years old, 5 feet, 7 and 3/4 inches tall, and weighs 345 pounds and 9 ounces, and has a bushy beard, hauls his bulk onstage, affecting a crab-step in an effort to squeeze between the grand piano positioned at the top of the stairs and the glowing maw of the orchestra pit. His gaze remains riveted on the cast, his broad back pressing against and following the gentle curve of the piano while raising his right arm, perhaps to give directions, and to anyone watching the gesture it only seems to draw attention to the Fat Man's feet, which suddenly appear too small to compensate for this slight shift in weight displacement. The body of the Fat Man now halts its sideways movement between the piano and the orchestra pit and teeters a moment on the edge. His mouth opens. The pianist rises from his stool and leans forward over the piano top, one hand managing a grab-hold on the Fat Man's shirttail. A few of the taller instruments, visible over the top of the pit, move toward the opposite end of the hollow, away from the looming mass of the Fat Man and the silent tug-o-war taking place above. The mouth of the Fat Man, open for the last few moments, clamps shut now as his gaze leaves the stage and travels a course around and down to the clamour of shuffling instruments below his feet. The grip of the pianist, hands weakened by hours of rehearsal, falters, and with an unceremonious grunt the director topples forward into the pit, landing on the tuba player and killing him instantly.

1

Big Guns and Peashooters

B UT THAT WAS on Saturday. On Friday morning, Sam Labovic (stints in Millhaven Pen, Springhill Institution and Sainte-Ame-des-Plaines), who is 51 years old, 5 feet, 11 inches tall, and weighs 185 pounds, 7 ounces, sits in Room 22 of the Niagara Hotel on Pender Street, fiddling with the dismantled pieces of a lightweight Commander Colt .45 automatic. His fingers move slowly, unrushed. Outside the window and across the street are a restaurant, a bookstore, and a stairway leading down to a print shop beneath the street. A gaudy neon sign of a waterfall hangs off the side of the hotel for the length of about three floors and is just visible outside his window. Deposits of oil spot the bedspread. Steely-blue parts from the lightweight Commander Colt litter the bed and reflect the dull November light coming through the window. From a small lamp on the bedside table, a weak half-circle of yellow light struggles its way through a cracked burnt linen hardback shade. The lightweight Commander Colt .45 is a good piece for Sam Labovic. He doesn't like heavy hardware. Too restricting. Unwieldy. Big guns can also make you feel like a common criminal, a thug no less. But, at the same time, no one wants to be stuck holding a peashooter either. "Every handgun is a compromise for the work needed," Sam Labovic is fond of saying, and the lightweight Commander Colt .45 weighs in at only twenty-seven ounces but is still nosed with a 7 and 7/8-inch barrel for accuracy. And what Sam Labovic likes best about the lightweight Commander Colt .45, what he likes best is the extra shot. Seven rounds instead of the old-time standard of six. That extra round, as Sam Labovic will be the first to admit, probably doesn't make a bit of difference these days with all the automatic weapons, but as far back as the Saturday cowboy matinees of his youth, he's been conditioned to think of handguns as holding only six rounds or less, and it's okay to hope the guys on the other side have watched those same matinees. Besides, for Sam Labovic, a firearm isn't for shooting; it's just an intimidator, a persuader. "If you gotta shoot, shoot the fucking ceiling or the floor, not at people or the walls," he tells those working with him.

"Shoot at the wall and it can be too easily construed that you're trying to shoot at someone, and, as for actually shooting at someone, that's not what the game is all about."

He stops fiddling with the Colt and taps the ash from his cigarette meticulously into the hotel ashtray beside the bed. His clothes lie neatly in the dresser drawers and his shaving kit is laid out with precision on the dresser top. For Sam Labovic, there is still some dignity to be had from performing the lesser tasks of one's existence with aplomb, keeping things neat and orderly and not letting it all go to the dogs. On the floor beside the bed, toes pointing out and aligned, are a pair of newly polished toe-cap British tan Oxfords with breathable uppers (can last a guy five or six years easy if cared for properly).

It's a bit chilly in the room, with low cloud and drizzle outside and the heater along the wall groaning occasionally like a small ship wallowing in heavy seas. He had worked the ships at one time when he was younger; saw Hong Kong, Melbourne, and Singapore. Other places. Worked all kinds of jobs when not practicing his true calling, attempts at toeing the line, going straight, his best chance was maybe the logging camp up Prince Rupert way where he had lived with the woman and the boy. He had taken to the small-town mentality and pace: the weekends camping by the lake, bear tracks pooling along the water's edge, the call of yellow-billed loons and the sudden burst of mallards spooking from the rushes and high reeds, where he showed the boy how to cast into the shadows of the shoreline pools, the hiss of the line trailing out, swish of the rod cutting the air, the laugh and shout of the boy when the strike came, rod jerking in his small hands, the silver-blue-pink flash of the fish breaking the smooth slick of the lake surface. Yes, that was the best time, all those four years ago. And damned if he'll ever know how and why it ended. And he's equally sure that if he did know, he'd know all that there ever was to know about anything. But, as things are, everything just seems to roll up into a big misty ball of time and memory, the ball growing larger, the mist, mistier.

Someone passes in the hall, making eerie shadows under the door. Muffled voices can be heard from the other side of the wall, arguing about something it sounds like, conflict of relationships, coming to terms. These sounds and shadows don't help things; he isn't sleeping well these days. And he wonders some more about the woman and the boy, how they're doing, if when the kid's grown he'll stay with the small town and the logging camps or succumb to the lure of the city. He hopes the kid stays in the bush; the city would be no good for him. The heater groans—another ship wallowing in heavy seas—as he reassembles the lightweight Commander Colt, fingers working competently.

* * *

As Sam Labovic reassembles his Colt automatic in Room 22 of the Niagara Hotel on Pender Street, Jorgen Thrapp is staring back at Kenny the printer in the print shop, the entrance of which is visible from Sam's hotel room across the street. Kenny is shuffling stacks of paper on the sorting table. A sour smell of chemicals pervades the place. Jorgen Thrapp works his fingers dexterously, flipping a monkey wrench into the air and catching it in turn.

"Look, man," says Kenny the printer. "I think it's just getting too hot with this stuff. Bernie wouldn't shit me."

"Bernie wouldn't shit you?" says Jorgen Thrapp, who is 29 years old, 5 feet, 11 and 1/2 inches tall, and weighs 149 pounds and 3 ounces. "How the hell you know Bernie wouldn't shit you?"

"Come off it Jorgen, why should he?"

The wrench lashes the air. "Why the shit wouldn't he shit you?"

"Aw, christ. He just wouldn't."

"How you know that?"

"I just know it."

"You don't know shit."

"Aw, christ—"

"Look man, I just need one more bundle of sheets, then I'm done," says Jorgen Thrapp. "The bettin' guys are all over fucking town for the game, money's flying around like crazy. They're insane. What's the problem? We're cashing in. Bernie may be a friend of yours but he's still a cop."

"It's not just the numbers, Jorgen. It's the other shit too."

"Other shit? What other shit?"

"You know what shit."

"I know what shit?"

"Oh, shit, man."

Some sheets of paper fall to the floor and Kenny the printer moves slowly to pick them up. "The drug shit, man. All that drug shit you got going. Bernie says they may be watching you. You even look a little stoned now."

"I'm never stoned, man. I'm level. And I say what does Bernie know?"

"He hears things, Jorgen. He should know."

"Bernie doesn't know shit."

"Oh, christ."

Jorgen Thrapp walks a circle, raising his hands. "Okay. Okay, I won't do anymore of that other shit until after the game. But will you please do the sheets? Christ, they've got those fucking lotteries. This is no big deal!"

"I just don't want any heat on the drug thing, man."

Jorgen Thrapp stops moving. "Don't worry, okay? Just do the sheets. Just this time. This is easy cash we're talking here Kenny. Easy cash. I mean, lookit that crap you're printing there. Wow. Real big bucks. What are they, menus or somethin'? Dipstick price lists? Wedding invitations? My numbers sheets are saving your ass."

"Okay, okay. I'll drop them at the same place."

"This afternoon."

"Yeah, this afternoon."

"*All right.*"

There's a loud *prang!* as the monkey wrench bounces off a pipe along the ceiling, rebounding down and narrowly missing the glass top of the light table.

"Jesus, Thrapp!"

"Look out!"

"Will you just get out of here?"

Jorgen Thrapp climbs the stairs, turning at the top to give Kenny the printer the nod. He hits the street, hurrying off. He's not happy. It's obvious that Kenny is losing his nerve, getting old or something. All this fuss. And Bernie the cop and all his shit. Why would the cops be watching him, Jorgen Thrapp? Who the hell was he to them? What he does is so small-time. Running numbers. Selling a few caps of this, a few tabs of that. Not worth the bother to bust this boy. Not even worth a citation or an ass-kiss from the captain. There are so many worse, bigger, and meaner fish in the sea.

He dons his reflector sunglasses, scurrying down Richards Street a few blocks to Robson, then turning right. A long fucking way to go just for some eats, he thinks, but Ron's the boss and wants what he wants from where he wants it. Further west along Robson, then he ducks into the restaurant-deli and pulls a crumpled scrap of paper from his pocket. The guy behind the take-out counter stares back at his reflection from Jorgen Thrapp's sunglasses. He recognizes the skinny geek as an almost-regular and considers him a bit of an ignoramus, always having to read his orders off scraps of paper. But it doesn't bother him; people are annoying in general and you get all kind of weirdos in this part of town. Jorgen Thrapp, on the other hand, feeling slightly notorious behind his reflector sunglasses and in charge after his talk with Kenny the printer, is bothered, trying to read his note.

"Vangoal Orega-something. To go."

"*Vangole Oreganata*," says the guy behind the counter.

"No kidding," says Jorgen Thrapp. "And what the fuck exactly is that, if you don't mind me asking."

"Don't mind," says the deli guy. "Baked clams with bread crumbs and some spices."

"Clams? Jesus. For lunch?"

The deli guy doesn't answer, moving off to the kitchen. Jorgen Thrapp waits, the toes of size-twelve Adidas tapping, palms beating on the countertop. And ol' Ron must think he's some kind of king shit connoisseur of something to be eating this kind of fuck-fancy stuff.

Polished Toe-cap British Oxfords

2

Worded Warnings

A s Jorgen Thrapp orders food to go and contemplates the validity of fuck-fancy food for lunch, half a mile away at City Hall, the intercom on Ms. Gibson's desk intones with the rich voice of Walter 'Dusty' Moons, the first black mayor of Vancouver.

"Ms. Gibson, could you come in here a moment, please?"

Ms. Gibson, with notepad and daybook and a pen with "Consulship of Greater Vancouver" stamped in white letters along its side, enters the Mayor's office. Mock-neck marled-yarn earth-toned sweater, lined print skirt. Mild scent of perfume. The dark face of Dusty Moons looks back at her from behind the desk through a thick blue haze of cigarette smoke. She quickly shuts the door behind her.

"Mr. Moons . . ."

"I know, Ms. Gibson. Smoking bylaw and all that. But I remind you, Ms. Gibson. It's the building that's public. This office is private. It says so right on the door."

"Yes, Mr. Moons."

"My appointments for the next few days, Ms. Gibson. A little tense today, Ms. Gibson. Let's keep it simple."

"Yes, Mr. Moons." She opens her daybook. "Let's see. Luncheon today with the Skirtell Women's Auxiliary in the boardroom. They'll be representing other related groups around the city in regards to control of festivities during the close of Grey Cup week. Then this afternoon, a final meeting with Police Chief Bellencamp on plans for security at the Grey Cup game on Sunday, and more urgently, the escalating party atmosphere now prevalent at some of the downtown hotels as they continue to fill up with fans for the game. He's sent along a report citing the necessity of dispatching thirty extra police to assist in quelling a 'rodeo' that was being held at two o'clock this morning in the main lobby of the Hyatt Regency."

"Rodeo, Ms. Gibson?" Dusty Moons says, blinking.

"Yes, Mr. Moons. Appears there was a live calf involved."

"Jesus christ," says Dusty Moons.

"Then tomorrow night," continues Ms. Gibson, "there's a dinner with the Grey Cup Steering Committee followed Sunday morning with the Grey Cup Parade to the stadium that you'll be riding in with the Premier and the CFL Commissioner, and following that the Premier has requested that you perform the ceremonial kick-off at one o'clock to start the game."

"*Jesus* christ," says Dusty Moons, taking on a panicky look. "I thought he was going to do that."

"I don't know, sir."

"Of course you don't, Ms. Gibson. But, as you *do* know, Ms. Gibson, where my people come from originally, fanaticism in the Caribbean tends to lend itself to tribal, religious, or political matters. We've had little time for the idolatry of sports. I have an Honours degree in Political Science, Ms. Gibson. And was captain of the debating team. I don't particularly like, watch, or know anything about the intrigues of the lofty pastime of North American football. I've seen kick-offs, Ms. Gibson. A man advances slowly to the ball, and he kicks it fifty yards, Ms. Gibson."

"I'm sure you're not expected to kick it fifty yards, Mr. Moons. I think it's just a symbolic gesture."

"Symbolic, Ms. Gibson? Of what, pray tell?"

"I'm not sure, sir."

A sigh, a black hand waving through the smoke. "Exactly. What else, Ms. Gibson."

"And also, sir, Sunday night the opera season opens at the Queen Elizabeth Theatre with Sophia Fugeta again in *La Traviata*." Ms. Gibson closes her daybook.

"The opera season? Sophia Fugeta?" An expression of

happy surprise etches itself on the until-now anguished face of Dusty Moons. Fingers drum an impromptu rhythm on the desktop. They stop to crinkle papers. His eyes enlarge somewhat and rove over the desk, travelling up to the book shelves along the walls—*The Seven Pillars of Wisdom* by T.E. Lawrence, *Nutrition Almanac*, *The Moral Compass* by William J. Bennett—and back down and around, over to the drapes, to the windows and out, to freedom, flight, and back to the desk and a notepad, the top sheet scrawled with obscene doodles which he now slips under the Transit Ledger.

"Is there anything else, Mr. Moons?" Ms. Gibson says gently, rising from her chair. "And don't forget, lunch with the Skirtell Women's Auxiliary tomorrow."

"Do you know, Ms. Gibson, what it's like being black *and* mayor?"

"No, I—"

"It's like being two minorities, Ms. Gibson. The shit it just flies and flies. I'm sorry, Ms. Gibson, I don't mean to upset you. As I've told you many times before, you're a pleasure to work with. A fine secretary and a true friend, Ms. Gibson. A veritable pillar of strength, a potency in the offices of the city consulship, Ms. Gibson."

"Thank you—"

"I will be leaning very heavily on you these next few days, Ms. Gibson. A loyal friend is a strong defense. The consulship of this fine city must stand strong, Ms. Gibson,

assured and solid . . . fearless and undismayed by any consequence, however inexplicable the consequence itself may
be, such as the event that occurred in the darker hours of
this morning at the Hyatt Regency Hotel. I will be relying
on your support, Ms. Gibson, part of which will be to keep,
if at all possible, trouble-makers away from that very door
marked 'Private' behind you. Until Monday at least. Protect
this black ass, Ms. Gibson, and it shall be grateful."

A flush rises up the throat of Ms. Gibson.

"That's all for now, Ms. Gibson."

"Yes, Mr. Moons . . ."

"Oh, one more thing, Ms. Gibson. Just what is it like out
there right now?"

"Out there, sir?"

"Yes, Ms. Gibson. Out there." Dusty Moons jabs a thumb
over his shoulder to the window.

"Well, Mr. Moons, Grey Cup week is always—"

"Ms. Gibson."

"A little . . . testy, Mr. Moons."

"A little *testy*, Ms. Gibson?"

"Yes, a little testy, Mr. Moons."

"Thank you, Ms. Gibson."

"Of course, Mr. Moons."

Dusty Moons, who is 53 years old, 5 feet 6 inches tall,
and weighs 172 pounds, lights another cigarette. The word
"testy" is whispered three times. On the desk, among the
many bits and slips of papers and memos, is a note marked

"Urgent" from Police Chief Bellencamp, uncovered when concealing the sheet of obscene doodles from the eyes of Ms. Gibson. It suggests bumped-up security around the actual Grey Cup cup itself, presently stowed under lock and key in a glass cage in the stadium offices. And a worded warning that the esteemed silvery chalice was indeed once stolen and held for ransom some many years back in Toronto, proving a source of monumental embarrassment for some other poor bugger called Mayor of that city.

3

Boneheads

Harry Pazik, who is 42 years old, 5 feet, 7 and 5/8 inches tall, and weighs 187 pounds even, pulls his two chins in above his shirt collar and grins into the mirror of Room 414 of the Hyatt Regency Hotel on Burrard Street in downtown Vancouver. He fumbles to adjust the large gold clasp fashioned in the horns of a steer that secures the western-style bolo tie at his neck. In the gold triangle between the horns, engraved in bold letters, is the name "Hank." And dangling down, out and over his stomach, are the two ends of the cords, capped with silver knobs fashioned in the hooves of a steer.

And it's no secret that Harry Pazik loves this tie, loves it as much as anything Harry Pazik loves in this world. Even, as Harry Pazik himself will admit, as much as his snakeskin Tony Lama cowboy boots inlaid with jade on the toes, purchased in El Paso, Texas. And, even, he'll admit, even as much as one might love one's wife and, yes, even as much as one might love one's own children. As much as one might love a large ranch-style home on the banks of the Bow River just outside of Calgary, and even—yes, even—as much as Calgary itself. As much as Alberta and the other provinces, as much as the whole effing country, by god. In fact, he may even love this tie as much as the Calgary Stampeders football team. Even as much as them.

And Harry Pazik loves them. Has them by fourteen points, taking the odds from what can only be called the screwballs, the non-believers, and the uninformed. It was all just money in the bank for anyone who knew what was what. In fact, the whole Vancouver trip could well be paid for from the winnings and still some left over. It wasn't really even gambling. Not when it was such a sure thing.

He cinches up the bolo. Behind him in the mirror, on a good day, would be a view of the harbour and North Shore Mountains. This late-November day, however, all is shrouded in low-lying cloud. West Coast weather, he's heard, can stay like this for months. It can get very depressing.

But Harry Pazik is anything but depressed. It's Grey Cup week and what a week it's been. Sure the game still has to be played, everyone knows that, but isn't that really just a formality? Isn't it all just a question of there being no question? The Grey Cup Championship has already been decided, as far as Harry Pazik is concerned. All save the weeping and moaning of the Eastern Conference fans. And as Harry Pazik has many times expounded in the local Vancouver bars over the past few days, the Toronto Argonauts, Eastern Champs, are playing with a rookie quarterback no less, a Bogdan *Michaldo* or something, for god's sake. What kind of a name is that for a quarterback?

He smiles a self-satisfied smile into the large panel mirror of Room 414 of the Hyatt Regency. On the six-drawer cherry laminate dresser is a neat pile of betting sheets, purchased just this morning while passing through the lobby from a weird skinny geek with mirrored sunglasses. A glass half-full sits atop the small bureau nearby, the sweet-sour smell of Canadian Club whisky. Posted on the wall beside the mirror, a notice offers "Soothing Finnish Massages" at the Hyatt's fully equipped health club, 8 a.m. to 10 p.m. There's also Dial-A-Prayer from the Unity Church of Truth, and, Harry presumes, if that one fails, a listing below it for Dial-A-Devotion at the Long Branch Baptist Church. The latter one appeals, the name being more akin to some image of the West, an image to which Harry Pazik two years ago surrendered himself whole-heartedly.

"Toronto," he announced to his own reflection. "You poor city-slicker boneheads. Can't even build a railway station."

This last remark, obscure at best to most people, alludes to Union Station on Toronto's Front Street, originally built to accommodate the Canadian Pacific Railroad and referred to through the years by Harry Pazik Senior when voicing his dislike of Torontonians—the station being unfit for use for eight years after completion due to the tracks, or was it the station, being laid in the wrong place.

None of this behaviour is to say that Harry Pazik Junior is a man of the West, a country boy and man of the plains. On the contrary, Harry Pazik Junior is by all rights an Easterner himself, raised plump and round in the middle-class areas of Ottawa, the nation's capital, and, as Harry Pazik Senior constantly reiterated, ("Home to such high-tech giants as Nortel, Tundra, and Cisco, Harry boy! Thirty museums! Fifty or so art galleries!") and so on. And father and son have both attained the popular accoutrements over time, on the outside anyway, that are considered indicative of a successful and happy life. ("For a man worth his salt, anyway," as Harry Pazik Senior so often exalted in putting it.) Harry Pazik Senior holds some post in government, although it's never been clear to Harry Pazik Junior exactly what that post is, but even at an early age he became aware that it suited the general ambiance of life in the capital that no one was ever really sure of what roles anyone else played in its governmental workings and that it was generally suspected that if everyone did know everyone else's roles, the entire structure would somehow crumble. Such has been the handed-down ideology throughout his growing years, so it's likely to remain with him, now primping himself in Room 414 of the Hyatt Regency, for all his years to come.

His first forty-three years have passed, and not without a reasonable and socially acceptable share of ups and downs (but, thankfully, no true suffering), one of which was a transfer two years ago with the Borthwick and Brodson Realty Company to the province of Alberta and the city of Calgary (to a life on the "perpetual and timeless frontier of this great country," as Harry Pazik Senior then put it), and the proud ownership of a ranch-style home on the Bow River. ("That cerulean ribbon on the gilded plain."—Harry Pazik Sr. again.)

So Harry Pazik Junior and family had moved west, Harry at least taking like a bee to honey to the self-styled image of the urban cowboy in both mind and attire. Cowboy boots, the Tony Lamas, were purchased on a trip to El Paso. A white Stetson worn almost daily, followed by the ranch-cut suits and belts with buckles of bucking broncos, crossed six-guns, or the stylized horns of the longhorn steer. And it's apparent even early on that the local populous seems more inclined to buy overpriced homes from cowboys, however epidemic, than ex-economics majors of Carleton University. And while much of life in Ottawa naturally concerned affairs of state (and so of money), however unclear, out west it was more oil and real estate—but still of money—and much clearer.

And there was sport.

The sport thing was new, particularly football. Well, not new, but the fanaticism was. There had been a passing interest in hockey at the Pazik household throughout his childhood, with Harry Pazik Senior always voicing support of the Montreal Canadiens or, in later years, the Ottawa Senators, if for no other reason than to illustrate his emphatic dislike of Torontonians. But Harry Pazik Senior rarely, if ever, attended a game, and, as a result, neither did Harry Pazik Junior. It was more of a social ploy, to have something other than the weather, or, more importantly, politics, to talk about at the many civil dinners and political functions that always in some way attempted to define Harry Pazik Senior's role in the bureaucratic scheme of things, but always failed to do so. Then came that first game out with the boys from the new Calgary office: Herb, Teddy, and Sid. McMahon Stadium. Hot rums from the Thermos. And Harry Pazik Junior was caught. To belong, to be a part of something, a great homogenous throng of one's fellows bound inexorably by one common cry: GO STAMPS GO! And on that first outing the Calgary Stampeders, ironically enough, were playing Ottawa, and Harry Pazik Junior found at last something tangible in life with which perhaps to oppose Harry Pazik Senior (safely, at least); on his feet in the stands, waving his Thermos, cap and scarf, red and white colours, and cheering for the Stamps. The West. And, of course, Harry Pazik Junior.

And from that first game, the devotion grows. Celia Pazik dutifully keeping the kids out of the way on weekend afternoons so Harry and the boys can watch the games unencumbered in the "game room" at the far end of the house. And it's during these times, happily ensconced on the tan vinyl recliner under the hand-picked prints of cattle drives and sun-darkened cowboys marauding through cheaply painted dust clouds, and Calgary Stampeder memorabilia and souvenirs hung in the game room—the one room in the house Harry Pazik Junior decorated entirely by himself—it's during these times that Harry Pazik Junior at last feels the slow inexorable emergence of a raw and completely personal identity. So it's not surprising that when the Calgary Stampeders win the Western title that Harry Pazik is the first to sign up for the Borthwick and Brodson Realty Company's charter-flight package to Vancouver to attend Grey Cup week and all its festivities. The week that ends on Sunday with the big game, seats on the forty-yard line, and, of course, an indomitable faith in the outcome.

And what a week it's been, since the arrival late last Monday night of one happy Harry Pazik, with Herb, Teddy, and Sid, Ralph Hogg and the Shapiros, and others of the gang of Borthwick and Brodson. And while being greeted by the red hotpants, white Stetsons, and high white boots of the hostesses in the main lobby of the Hyatt Regency, Harry Pazik does silently offer thanks to whatever Powers That Be for this, the greatest of times. And thanks Them again that Mrs. Pazik hates football almost as much as she hates his friends, and has chosen to stay home with the kids.

So it's with these happy thoughts and emotions that Harry Pazik Junior now dresses himself in front of the large panel mirror of Room 414 of the Hyatt Regency in downtown Vancouver and remembers not the Harry Pazik who moved out to life on the perpetual and timeless frontier of this great country only two (or is it three?) years ago. This Harry Pazik is now a better man, a man with his own private room with a view, when the weather provides, of the Vancouver harbour and mountains, even a small balcony, individual climate control, dataport outlets to everyone and everything, a mini-bar that's hardly mini and seats waiting on the forty-effing-yard line. And a man with something better than that. A man with something better than a lot of things. This is a man with, literally, something to cheer about.

The fire alarm clangs in the outer hallway, and Harry Pazik Junior is at once airborne above the roseate-flush carpet of Room 414 of the Hyatt Regency, glass of Canadian Club in hand, whisky trickling up a sleeve. And in the same movement he heads for the phone by the bed.

"Hello? Desk? Look. The alarm thing again. Is this one the real thing or another gag? Look, can't you guys do anything about this? This has got to be the hundredth alarm I've heard since I've been here. You guys could get sued. The Calgary fans? Not much you can do? I see."

Phone down, he refills his glass.

Boneheads. Every effing Calgary fan in town must be

staying at the Hyatt. One would think everyone was back in high school, for christ's sake. Next thing someone'll be pissing off the roof or something. The only really good thing anyone's done is taken a branding iron—where they heated it up is anyone's guess—and burned some ranch insignia on the wall of the men's john in the lobby.

"The lid has to blow," thinks Harry Pazik. "With this kind of craziness, the lid has got to blow."

He moves back across the room, bed unmade, a few empty and partially empty liquor bottles complementing the empty and partially empty beer cans. Piles of partially eaten and gnawed chicken bones, in their part, complement the partially eaten and gnawed bones of honey-garlic ribs. Some gleam up from the carpet, complementing the sparkles gleaming down from the chintzy stucco ceiling. And all of it seems to complement Harry Pazik, silver hooves dangling off his belly as he pulls a western-cut sports coat over his shoulders and shakes down the sleeves. The final touch: the white Stetson plunked over his head.

In cowboy boots he stands a full five-nine, and with the Stetson he zooms to over six feet. The overall effect is damn satisfying, although he does notice, a little unhappily, that it wouldn't hurt to partake, at some unspecified time in the future, in some form of legitimate exercise. And this joint does have your high-end health club full of treadmills and fitness machines, whirlpools, and aerobic classes, but who in their right mind would use any of that on a vacation?

"Bowling isn't exercise," Celia's always saying.

Damn. He was supposed to call.

A pounding on the door, and he hears Herb and Sid shouting from the hallway, another haymaker about to begin. Harry Pazik searches for his wallet and room card, high-steps around the beer cans and chicken bones, then pausing at the door to gulp the rest of the whisky, the fire alarm rages once more—for the hundredth-and-first effing time—and more whisky splashes to the carpet and more trickles up his sleeve. And it occurs to Harry, at this precise moment, that this is definitely not a convenient time to phone home and chat, cell phone tossed onto the bed at the last moment before the door to Room 414 of the Hyatt Regency Hotel in Vancouver closes behind him.

Sorry, Celia.

4

Dance of de Demons

JORGEN THRAPP SLINKS down the hallway in the basement of the Queen Elizabeth Theatre, unsaddled for the moment of the responsibility of running errands for Ron Kanavrous, the lighting designer, and Kristy Kibsey, the stage manager, who are upstairs this very minute in the theatre proper, running through the lighting of *La Traviata* with the Fat Man. A high-speed ticking, like a large frenzied insect, resonates over an industrial hum as he enters the boiler room. Something clanks sporadically from an unknown source where two components of machinery occasionally meet out of whack. He advances cautiously through the gloom to the tiny door marked MAINTENANCE and unlocks it. His arm reaches its way around and inside from the safety of the doorway to flick on the light. A dim lightbulb blinking from the centre of the ceiling exposes a clutter of mops, buckets, and brooms, dusty shelves replete with a confusion of fuses, wire coils, cords, boxes of nails, nuts, screws, and bolts. A welding tank in one shadowy corner sits next to a large gallon jar hand-labelled: Unknown Solution—Do Not Drink. A musty odour, like old clothes punctuated with the tangy smell of chemicals, reminds him of Kenny's print shop. He moves forward, feet kicking things out of the way, and bends over, his hands digging down behind an unappealing pile of old rags and paint cans and coming up with a battered padlocked tackle box. He hunches over, fingers fumbling through a maze of keys from his belt chain. Throughout, he has kept up a muttered conversation with himself.

"Okay . . . Valium, fives and tens for Sandra and Denise . . . Percocet and Fiorinal for Howard, that space cadet . . . Demerol for Ronny boy . . . some simple codeine-rich 292s—jesus, real drug fiend—for poor unlaid Kristy . . ."

The lid of the tackle box comes open, revealing an impressive collection of tiny bottles and plastic baggies in a bright array of colours, a personal pharmaceutical rainbow of abirritants to the stings of life. Under the top tray lies a cavity filled with bills of various denominations and betting sheets—these, too, organized by colour—and he begins sifting through the bottles and baggies, pausing with some to check the label and put them aside.

And screw Kenny, he thinks. And Bernie the cop, that shit-ass. Just over forty-eight hours before opening night of the opera season and he should cool it? Those bozos obviously don't know theatre people. Neurotic psychotic. Or some-thing. No one can handle it, opening night. The last-minute jeebies, the changes and catastrophies that are bound to occur when so many stressed-out creative-type-psychos try to coordinate to one end. The whole human race is built like that, nutballs, bouncing off the freaking wall. Ups and downs, gentlemen. No one can handle it. At least, no one without the help of the Jorgen Thrapps of this world.

He replaces the tiny bottle labelled Benzedrine, then shrugs his shoulders and picks it up again, removes the cap and pops some tabs in his mouth. And does the same with the Talwin, three or four of these babies, everyone at one time or another needs a boost. He crams the other pills to fill orders into his pockets, grabs a small bundle of betting sheets. Definitely running low on these; Kenny the printer had better come through. Opportunity was passing them by, time and money a-wasting. Everyone deserves some sort of better—well, most everyone—well, one at least.

At the sound of the boiler room door opening, the bottom of Jorgen Thrapp's stomach seems to drop to somewhere around his knees. His hands have always trembled, a natural phenomenon he would argue, but now they shake violently. His jaw, also known to tremble on occasion, drops open like the hinged tab on a bubblegum machine.

Cops! he decides.

No way! he argues.

And why the fuck not? he questions.

It's an unconscious nervous reaction, gobbling the pills still in his hand, straightening and facing the tiny doorway of the maintenance room. To make a move now could spell disaster. His thoughts chatter back and forth over each other—the voice of his mother when he was a child, hell, the voice of his mother—*Jorgen, dere are punishments for dose who stray.* His father—*Jorg, I don't know what get into you, god know I try. You waver from de path, you like de self-destruction, de dance of de demons? Tobogganing down dis hill of craziness an' bad tings—*

Christ, enough of that. Dad was a claims adjuster, not a fucking prophet. Did a lot of fires. Often a faint scent of damp smoke and old ash wafted from his clothes while peering across the kitchen table over a copy of the *Aravot Daily,* the Armenian newspaper he faithfully subscribed to. Looking that look: half anger, half pleading. Somewhere along the line, he and Mom had combined (what seemed to Jorgen) various forms of Christianity and Catholicism into their own evangelical religion-type-thing that had an idiom for every ill and a no-holds-barred nasty ass-biting outcome for all those, who, as his mother too often pointed out, had "strayed."

Yes, he can remember the possible ills along the road that may have caused him to stray a bit, like getting punched out frequently in the school yard, being relentlessly bullied through the early grades and flunking the important exams and then trying to turn it all around by trying to feel up Stephanie Ann Demello behind the bleachers, a move to make him cool, one of the guys. From there a veritable kaleidoscope of unacceptable behaviour mixed with a declining percentage of the acceptable, each episode of the unacceptable inevitably leading up to what he has come to refer to simply as The Story. One has always some time to think up The Story, to cover what one has just screwed up. To make the real stuff go away and leave a pleasant illusion in its place, an untrue but at least intelligent rendering of what one has done (well, not done), and why one did it (well, why one did something he didn't really do). And it is true that The Dream has returned of late, although he's never been sure if it's supposed to bode good or ill. The Owl-guy dream. Since his childhood it comes and goes: an image, primitive, of a man-shape, large round eyes, round head (no hair), standing with one arm pointed skyward, the other to the ground, feet like talons. And sometimes it evokes fear, sometimes it feels friendly, protective. In Grade 11, his last year before dropping out, while studying unexplained phenomenon in Mr. Shepherd's science class, he found a photo in a textbook, the Owl-guy of his dreams. Almost an exact likeness looking up from page 122, Chapter 11.

"Mr. Shepherd?"

"Ah, young Mr. Thrapp."

"This picture here . . ."

"Ah, the Nazca Plateau earth drawings, I see. Peru. Visible only from the air. Eighteen bird figures, I believe. A spider too, spanning one hundred and fifty feet or more. They're dug out in one continous line, did you know? Quite the mystery who did them or why. Or when for that matter . . ."

"But, this one, Mr. Shepherd."

"Ah, the Owl-man. Yes."

"He's . . . it's just that . . . ah . . . I've seen him in my dreams."

"Dreams, dear boy? You don't want to be doing that. These glyphs to the gods or whatever they are, not to be messed with, I should think."

And now, here, in the boiler room of the Queen Elizabeth Theatre, trying to cast aside any stupid and occult-type thinking, he has a horrible revelation—*Kenny the printer is probably right! Bernie that shit-ass does know! Everything!*

The footsteps have stopped just outside the maintenance room. Jorgen tenses with the sound. What is it? Something sliding on something, like revolver metal on holster leather; those fucking gung-ho cops already have their guns out! Hear these knees a-knockin', no, you can't come in. He should have stayed in school, followed those elusive dreams of success that pop stars sing about. Cut the bullshit chatter in your head, can hear someone breathing out there, just by the door. It can't be a SWAT team; impossible. But whoever it is seems to be waiting, getting set, psyching themselves up for the sudden rush and take-down of, he, the notorious

Jorgen Thrapp, most likely to be thrown face-down on the concrete maintenance-room floor, teeth bouncing into all four corners. And then there's jail, incarceration, if this really is the cops. The sheer humiliation, the folks appearing bewildered and tearful on the late-night news, the segment maybe taped in their own kitchen, Dad at the table with his copy of the *Aravot Daily* spread out before him, Mom standing in the background, pot of perogies steaming on the stove behind her while she wrings her white flour-dusted hands—"He vas always such a goot boy."

"Jorgen?"

At the sound of his name, the body of Jorgen Thrapp performs no mean feat gaining what seems seconds of airtime above the maintenance room floor. On landing, he manages to toss back the remaining assortment of pills still clutched in his other hand. Then there's only enough time to stare down at his now-empty palms in dull surprise and wonder, "God, what *were* those?" Kristy Kibsey stands tearful in the doorway, and with no rush of cops and no take-down and absolutely no cool left to lose, he lets go a cry of his own while slamming down the lid of the tackle box.

Kristy jumps.

Jorgen Thrapp jumps.

Kristy cries.

Jorgen Thrapp wraps his arms around himself. "For christ's sake, Kristy."

Kristy moans, "Ooooooh, Jorgen."

Jorgen Thrapp moans back, "Ooooooh, Kristy . . ." and his mind and body begin their dissolution into drug and adrenalin-induced chaos while his hands try vainly to stuff betting sheets into his pockets.

The Owl-man

5

Cawnrud Fawken Who?

DUSTY MOONS SMILES valiantly into the camera, his right hand grasping firmly that of Willy Brisco, the head coach of the Calgary Stampeders. Visible behind the photographer, the towering wall of the rest of the team stands puffing and perspiring from their recent practice, each sweat-streaked face with a smile of its own.

The first black mayor of Vancouver is not comfortable. The aroma of damp bodies encases him as he squirms against the closeness of the locker room. The showers keep up a strident hiss from somewhere behind the barrier of players, sending clouds of steam billowing along the ceiling. The cinder-block walls are painted a sickly pastel pink with snot-grey trim. He hopes the visible sheen on the walls is the high-gloss paint and that the cinder-blocks are not exuding sweat themselves.

He smiles at Willy Brisco. "Good luck, Mr. Brisco."

The beefy face of Willy Brisco grins back. "Thank you, Dusty, but luck won't have anything to do with it."

Dusty Moons holds his smile, thinks, Okay, fine, Mr. Brisco, may the best team win. Play the game and all that. The first black mayor of Vancouver does adhere to a philosophy of good sportsmanship, if somewhat plebeian, and there will be no humiliation for either side in defeat. All competition on the field of athletics is a noble endeavour and he is not here to take sides. Although, by all the gods and many ethereal spirits of his Caribbean forefathers, he is tempted.

A few more pictures are taken and the press shoot is over. The crowd of reporters disperses and Dusty Moons begins to make his way through the players, offering best wishes all around in the upcoming game. He is followed hesitantly by Mr. Dwyer, his aide. In the squeeze of the lockers, the hulking form of 'Mad Joe' Mezzaroba, defensive right guard who is 27 years old, 6 feet, 7 and 1/2 inches tall, and weighs 298 pounds, 2 and 1/2 ounces, suddenly looms above them. Dusty Moons gazes upward at a tangle of teeth, most of them chipped or missing, embedded in large pink gums. A large number 66 looks back at him from the front of a frayed red jersey, inches from his nose.

"Good practice, Mr. Mezzaroba?" He puts out his hand.

"Right on, Mistah Mayor." The huge taped meathook of Mad Joe engulfs his hand. Squeezes.

"Pleased," says Dusty Moons, unflinching. "Good luck tomorrow, Mr. Mezzaroba."

"Shit man. We dun' need no luck."

Dusty Moons again holds his smile. "Going to 'exterminate all the brutes' eh, Mr. Mezzaroba?" says Dusty Moons.

"Huh?"

Dusty Moons regrets his mistake. "Umm . . . *Heart of Darkness*, Mr. Mezzaroba. Conrad?"

"Cawnrud?"

A body is slammed into a locker door and there comes an explosion of catcalls and guffaws. Dusty Moons feels Mr. Dwyer shift uneasily at his side as a voice booms out.

"Yeah, Joe! Conrad!"

"Cawnrud fawken *who?*" drawls Mad Joe Mezzaroba.

Dusty Moons keeps his composure; he has a job to do. But it might be better to keep things simple and dispatch with the witticisms and literary references. Time to lower the tone. "Getting any, Mr. Mezzaroba?"

Loud slaps and poundings all around this time and a whoop, not directly a part of the conversation, soars from the showers.

"Day an' night, Mistah Moonie."

Haw-haw. Slam! Bam!

Jesus, his ears are taking a beating, and Dusty Moons wishes nothing more than to retrieve his hand from Mad Joe's and get the hell out of there.

"Ever play football, Mister Moonie?"

Dusty Moons senses danger; Mad Joe's dumb-boy accent seems to have disappeared. "No, I haven't, Mr. Mezzaroba. Not as you know it. A little soccer . . ."

"Oh yeah? Where at?"

"Oh, high school a bit. College. That's all."

"Bet you were a tiger."

More guffaws, bams and slams. He can feel Mr. Dwyer pressing even closer to his side and Dusty Moons accordingly presses an elbow gently but firmly into his ribs. Mr. Dwyer grunts and quits pressing.

"Ah . . . well, good luck, Mr. Mezzaroba." And shouting over the din—"Good luck to all!"

He turns, using the resisting body of Mr. Dwyer to run interference as the narrow packed space erupts in another explosion of slamming locker doors, guffaws, and piercing hoots. They reach the open space at the end of the lockers, only to confront again the meaty face of head coach Willy Brisco, this time with a fat cigar in his mouth.

"Have one Dusty. They cost a fortune. Havana."

"No thanks, Mr. Brisco. Too much for me I'm afraid."

"Making a hit with the boys, eh? Well, that's good, Dusty."

"Yes, a good bunch, Mr. Brisco."

"Kind of you to say, Dusty. That Mad Joe now. You know, he's got a goddamn Bachelor of Science or something. Just having a little fun an' all that."

"I'm sure, Mr. Brisco."

"You know, I don't usually smoke these things but, hell, we got it. Why not flaunt it, eh?"

"Got it, Mr. Brisco?"

"Call me Willy. Oil, Dusty. We got the oil!"

"Oh, yes."

"You know, people think us Albertans are pompous bastards 'cuz we got the oil. And we are. Why the hell not, eh? Make the rest of you think a bit, huh?"

"Yes. Yes, I guess it does."

"What you think of my boys? Mean lookin' lot, eh?"

"Should be a good game, I think."

"I don't want to sound, um . . . *pompous*, Dusty. Haw-haw. But I think we're gonna kick Toronto's collective asses."

Dusty Moons smiles pleasantly. "That you may do, Mr. Brisco, that you may do. But, you know, 'Willy,' the Greeks were drilling for oil as far back as 400 BC. And a lot of good it did them, in the long run, is all I'm saying."

"The Greeks? Hell, we'd kick their asses too."

Dusty Moons and Mr. Dwyer reach the locker room door, this time followed by the guffaws of Willy Brisco. At the door they turn back, one last nod and diplomatic smile of support and good will, just in time to see Mad Joe Mezzaroba standing his bulk atop a bench and saluting with a well-taped paw.

"DAY AN' NIGHT, MISTER MOONIE! DAY AN' NIGHT!"

Dusty Moons follows Mr. Dwyer up the stairs, and once outside proclaims: "That had all the charm of visiting a cave of Mithraics."

Mr. Dwyer dabs his face with a hanky, puffing clouds of steam into the chilly air. "The what, Mr. Moons?"

"Nothing, Mr. Dwyer. Suffice to say they were pagans who lived in caves and worshipped the bull, which they sacrificed frequently, revelling in the blood and gore more than their religion."

"I see," says Mr. Dwyer.

"Don't you though," says Dusty Moons.

They climb into the limousine, and Dusty Moons loosens his tie. On his lapel is a round shiny button of red and white: GO STAMPS GO. He removes it and tosses it out the window.

"I realize, Mr. Dwyer, that most football players, let alone other athletes, are highly intelligent. They must be to memorize all those plays or learn strategy or whatever, but . . ."

"Yes, Mr. Moons?"

"That 'Mad Joe' is quite the frigging buffoon *nonpareil*, Mr. Dwyer."

"So it would appear, Mr. Moons. And that Willy Brisco, if you don't mind me saying . . ."

"Yes, Mr. Dwyer?"

"Is a fucking bonehead, sir."

"Ah . . ."

6

Of What Life is Made

HARRY PAZIK GREETS Saturday morning in quiet alarm. Tremors, qualms, and jitters. His body aches and his nerve tissues course with anxiety. He lies on his side, arm dangling off the edge of the bed. His eyes refuse to discern distance or detail, lower intestine suddenly writhing like a python, and, being too weak to fight it, he lets the pressure burn itself out underneath the covers.

"Jesus, Harry!"

With the sound of these unexpected words in a voice not his own, his mind takes what he imagines is a high dive off some anonymous hundred-storey building, his bleary eyes staring wildly ahead at the hotel room curtains that cover the window, a mundane pattern of blurred pastel oval shapes, some overlapping, and, what do you know, making

different colours, a vertical fuzzy fissure of daylight wink-
ing back through the join in the drapes. What appears to be
raindrops are spotted against that tiny fissure of hotel room
glass, but no other clues. But that doesn't matter. Nothing
matters. Nothing matters but the voice. The voice and the
disconcerting odour seeping up from under the covers that
it's too late to do anything about, released in the first place
only because he thought he was alone. And the voice. Here
in Room 414 of the Hyatt Regency, where, at this time anyway, no other voices should be.

"Go to the bathroom if you have to, for god's sake."

Harry Pazik is silent, his hands now gripping the covers,
knuckles against his chin. And he refuses to roll over. Or
make inquiries.

"On second thought, I'll go first. Don't think I could stand
it." A weight leaves the bed. Footfalls across the carpet.

Harry Pazik lies still, as still as Mayor Dusty Moons will
soon sit in his city office across town, trying to establish pri-
orities. The daylight in the gap between the hotel room curtains appears to flutter with the closing of the bathroom
door. A sinking feeling in the gut, nausea maybe. He sees
himself as a young lad, at the Tulip Explosion floral show at
the Casino du Lac-Leamy during the Canadian Tulip Festival
back home in Ottawa, millions of tulips in their multitude of
colours, and being dragged along by his mother's hand, his
small nose touching those frosted pink tulip petals of huge
dimensions that bend down toward him as she chats with

someone she's met, and he's been feeling ill all day. A young boy's vomit then drips off the frosted pink tulip petals that appear to recoil as his mother yanks his hand, bends herself down in place of the tulip to say, "Harry, what in god's name?"

And now, in Room 414 of the Hyatt Regency in Vancouver, it seems again an appropriate question as an owl takes up its call in his head. *Who? Who? Who?* it asks.

He recoils further under the covers as the bathroom door opens. Footfalls come back and the weight returns to the bed.

"That's better."

The owl in his head going crazy. *Who? Who? WHO?*

The phone, not ringing—blasting.

Good god, and he stifles the owl that stifles a cry. The phone is on the other side of the bed. THAT side, where the voice is and the weight is shifting. The voice is picking it up, too late to stop it. And he knows—oh god, no—it can only be—

"Here, Harry."

And he now recognizes the voice, the voice of Dezura Shapiro. Dezura Shapiro, in bed with Harry Pazik in Room 414 of the Hyatt Regency Hotel on Burrard Street in Vancouver. Married to Roger Shapiro, who also works for the Borthwick and Brodson Realty Company and is also somewhere else in the Hyatt Regency Hotel on Burrard Street in Vancouver. Dezura Shapiro, who is 43 years old, 5 feet, 3 and 1/2 inches tall and weighs 133 pounds, 7 ounces with a 42 D-cup chest, the same Dezura Shapiro of batiks and abstract paintings, book clubs, pottery classes, foreign movies, and cooking all her meals in woks. And about the phone call—it can only be—oh, christ—what in god's name, Harry, was he doing?

Some relief then, suddenly realizing Dezura Shapiro has not actually spoken into the phone. He takes the receiver over his shoulder, still refusing to turn over. Maybe everything will go away. An unnerving glimpse of clothes, his own and others more brightly coloured, strewn about the floor. His and hers. And a dizzying recollection of the night before: a naked Dezura Shapiro, bare behind aimed like a cannon for firing at the heavens. And breasts, like hot air balloons snagged on lethal treetops, swinging below that. And above it all one grinning Harry Pazik Junior, poised, pants around his ankles.

Oh, lord momma.

He manages a feeble croak into the phone. "Hello?"

"Harry?" The voice of Celia Pazik. "Harry, is that you?"

Dezura Shapiro is a frantic whisper in his other ear. "Good god! Is that Roger?"

"Harry? Harry, are you there?"

His two ears seem to disconnect, straining to keep the two messages from meeting and hearing each other. He has an absurd fear that two distinctly separate sounds, maybe for this one time only, may actually enter through each opposing earway and meet in the middle, somewhere behind his eyes, and that the voice on the line can hear the incoming sordid secret from the other.

He says nothing.

The fingers of Dezura Shapiro pry the receiver out of his hand and replace it on the terminal. Thank you, dear lady. Then these same fingers pull the cord from the jack and roll his still form onto its back. Dezura Shapiro leans over him and hazards a quick check of his breathing and heart rate, this one-time nurse from Manitoba, and establishing that all is, if not well, not immediately life threatening either.

"You don't look at all well, Harry."

No reply.

"C'mon, Harry. Pull yourself together."

"Dezura" (squeaked). "Roger is a big man and a maniac. He'll kill me."

Dezura nods, sympathetic. "And Celia's not exactly tiny either, Harry. And she'll kill you too."

"Leave the phone off."

"It's disconnected."

"And make sure the door's locked."

"Take it easy, Harry. No one knows."

"The whole world knows. I know it."

"Jesus. Celia have a crystal ball or something?"

"All the women in Celia's family have proven powers. You've seen Celia's mother. How she can just appear with no warning . . ."

"Oh, christ. I gotta go."

"Dezura—what happened?"

"You don't remember?"

"Well, I remember—"

"I'm hurt, Harry."

"Don't be hurt, Dezura."

"Not *that* hurt. *This* hurt. My rump's still got the marks."

"Oh, god. Please don't tell Roger."

"Are you crazy? It's my butt too, you know."

And so it is, thinks Harry Pazik, so it is. The butt of Dezura Shapiro.

"Where're my things?"

"On the floor. There. Everywhere. Make sure you get everything."

"Jesus, Harry. Will you lighten up? Your voice is shaking."

"Leave discreetly. Is there a fire escape?"

"For god's sakes. Are you nuts? Maybe you want I should leave in a laundry hamper or something."

"It's an idea."

"Oh, christ."

Dezura Shapiro rummages through clothes on the floor—hot air balloons swinging—and finds her brassière. Naked and standing over the bed.

"Okay *girls*. Say goodbye to Harry."

His eyelids flutter, willing his eyeballs not to look. One eyeball rebels, manages a peek.

"If I had my way, Harry, I wouldn't wear one of these damn things. But Roger . . ."

"Some people call you a hippy, Dezura."

"Yes, I know. Eccentric. Crazy. Just because I read so much. And prefer going to art shows and foreign movies instead of drunken block parties and I haven't joined the Borth*dick* and Brodson Wives' Bowling Team. And I smoke a little dope."

"You smoke a lot of dope, Dezura."

"And just because I smoke a lot of dope."

"It's bad for you, Dezura."

She looks down at him—pityingly, he thinks.

"You don't look well, Harry. Love among the ruins." Her voice goes sing-song. "Where the quiet-coloured end of evening's smile . . . lust of glory pricked their dicks up, dread of shame struck them tame . . ."

"You making this up? It's not the time—"

"Just something I know, loosely translated. You alright?"

"I'll be okay. You better go."

"I'm going. I'm going."

"Oh, my god. That was Celia."

"Come my Celia, drink to me only with thine eyes . . ."

"It's not funny, Dezura."

"You should read more, Harry. It helps at times like this."

"Yes, I can see that."

"She'll call back."

"One can be sure."

"I hope you feel better, Harry."

"I will. There's only one direction to go from here."

"See? Optimistic already. Don't let the guilt kill you."

Dezura Shapiro, finally clothed, heads across the room. Whir of motion. Beaded vermillion top, long dress over high leather boots and silver hoops dangling from her ears, red sunglasses across her nose. And pauses at the door.

"I thought you guys were supposed to have a good time on these things."

"We do, we do. It's just that . . ."

"Roger's the same way. I look at you guys, Harry, and I wonder if you even know what you really want, even half the time. This is your big week, Harry, although for what exactly . . ."

"No philosophy, Dezura."

"Don't panic. I'm going. Keep your pecker up."

"Goodbye."

"Ciao."

The door of Room 414 of the Hyatt Regency closes, and the fissure of light at the window wavers. He remains still, trying not to think. But he does think. And what do you know, Dezura Shapiro. But for a small indiscretion, what a time, what a time one is having. The champs. The Stampeders are going to be the champs. Try to think about that. They're going to beat the boneheads. And this boy here will be taking home the glory and the dough from the side-bets. These singular occasions are of what life is made, Dezura Shapiro. After much hard work, setting goals and attaining them and earning these special times. Life is mapped with pinnacles and you better plant your flag, Dezura Shapiro. Fulfillment is not just another word for *keep your pecker up*. And you do look like a hippy, just like everyone says.

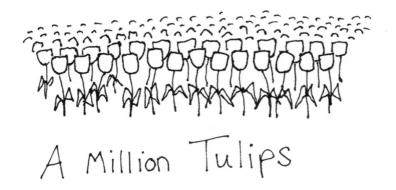

A Million Tulips

7

Nimrods

STEPPING OUT OF the lobby elevator, Dezura Shapiro makes directly for the main doors. From the main desk, the clerk watches with hooded eyes as she crosses the lobby carpet, unable as he is to relate her dress and manner to the rest of the Grey Cup groups that have invaded the hotel. She's part of that Calgary realty bunch and, though attractive in a way, it's hard to put a make on her through the beads, necklaces, scarves, and what appears to be a generally multicultural sense of fashion. But of one thing Mike Hatskill can be sure. Of one thing Mike Hatskill need have no doubts. And it's two things, really. It's those tits. Those tits are something else.

Another set of eyes, less hooded—in fact, wide open—stares out from the doorway of the administrative offices as Dezura Shapiro crosses the lobby floor. And it's the silent conclusion of the hotel manager, Merrill Swann, that Dezura Shapiro would be well worth a roll regardless of the severe dress, the pounds of bracelets, scarves, and assorted hoopla. And those tits could stand well enough alone through anything, a magnificent pair, evoking not only awe, but fear.

He pauses discreetly before emerging from the doorway; it doesn't do to appear obvious while ogling the female guests. Then he too crosses the lobby carpet, a man of missions, with a managerial dignified step. He notices a miniscule but annoying squeak from the heel of his right shoe when he walks—how in the hell?—and makes a mental note to change shoes at the first opportunity. Mike Hatskill catches the musky scent of Dragoon Noir cologne approaching and averts his eyes from the disappearing sight of Dezura Shapiro.

"Mr. Hatskill."

"Morning, Mr. Swann."

"And what's the good news?"

"Fairly quiet so far today, sir. Two more fire alarms pulled last night. That makes eleven since Monday."

"Jesus christ, Mr. Hatskill. Where *do* they come from?"

"Calgary, I think, sir."

"Yes. Well, I fear we're not out of the woods yet, Mr. Hatskill. One can feel the hysteria mounting. It's been like a snowball rolling down a mountainside and slowly gaining in size and momentum. And the fucking thing is rolling right at us, Mr. Hatskill."

"Yes, sir."

"Can't say it hasn't intrigued me, Mr. Hatskill, if one is interested in studying this kind of thing, people's multitude of diversions for fun and profit. As if putting a man on the moon isn't enough, we invent games to be played at the risk and peril of the participants— 'transposing our aggressions,' I think the psychologists call it—and then we do all in our power to injure, maim, and cold-cock ourselves in celebration of its glories."

"Yes, sir."

"And even those are questionable."

"Yes, sir."

"You a football fan, Mr. Hatskill?'

"Prefer hockey, sir."

"Ah . . ."

Merrill Swann lets his gaze drift a moment over the ordered sophistication of the hotel lobby. Comfortable rolled-arm club chairs, bevelled glass-top coffee tables. Tasteful prints of West Coast landscapes line the walls. In the centre, facing the main doors, is a large raised flowerbed of sorts, a kind of indoor arboretum, playing host to a variety of smaller trees and plants, all real. The lobby itself more like an atrium than a hotel lobby, opening for two storeys, where a promenade can be seen leading to the restaurant above. Pedestal tables occasionally sport a mock candelabrum or flowering plant. And he is always watchful for droopy vegetation, litter, and unlawful smoking.

Merrill Swann is proud of his station, enjoying the constant variety of people who continuously pass through the hotel. And he's never felt subservient as the manager of a hotel either, an employee in the "hospitality industry." Some do, but he's always accepted the importance of his role, and that role is to cater, mollify, and smooth the ruffles that are invariably inherent not only to travelling, but to existence in general. Having seen much and endured all in the business, he is nevertheless unable not to react as his gaze lights upon five ragged youths who enter through the main doors.

"Who, Mr. Hatskill, in god's name are they?"

Mike Hatskill scrolls down the screen in front of him, causing Merrill Swann a heightened agitation by tapping a fingernail rapid-fire against the monitor.

"Let's see . . . Butt Ugly, sir."

"Pardon, Mr. Hatskill?"

"Butt Ugly, sir. They're the band for tonight. The leader's name is . . . Dingo, sir."

"I see . . . and who—"

"Some of the Calgary group, sir. They booked them for tonight and tomorrow at special request. In the Plaza Ballroom upstairs, I think, sir."

"Let the band begin . . ." mutters Merrill Swann.

The five youths head for the elevators, which are set off from the lobby by a huge mirrored wall. Just before turning the corner they begin shoving, goofing off, one of them falling to the floor. They ogle their reflections.

Merrill Swann reaches into an inner breast pocket and removes a small vial. He shakes two pills into the palm of his hand, popping them into his mouth. His hand returns the vial to the breast pocket and comes back with a soft pearl-white hanky that dabs at his lips. "Now, Mr. Hatskill. Security all set for tonight?"

"Yes, sir."

"And remember, Mr. Hatskill. *No more fucking animals.* The people are enough. If it was a live calf-roping last night, god only knows what it could be tonight."

"Yes, sir."

"And how did they get the thing in here, I'd like to know."

"No idea, sir."

"And what of the 'brand' burnt into the wall of the men's washroom?"

"They're working on it, sir. Have to replace the tile."

"Kind of makes the merry pranks of college fraternities pale, doesn't it, Mr. Hatskill?"

"Yes, sir."

Merrill Swann looks at him thoughtfully. "Do you find all this amusing, Mr. Hatskill?'

"Not at all, sir."

"I mean, one could if it wasn't one's own ass, couldn't one?"

"I suppose, sir."

"Carry on, Mr. Hatskill."

"Yes, sir."

Merrill Swann once more surveys the lobby, preparing to leave. His ears attune to the steady murmur of voices as people move through, their voices for the most part kept low, as one would speak in, say, the hallowed halls of a church, or better, a cathedral. These are the moments, when all the machinery is working, when each guest is obeying the rules and protocol of respectability, these are the moments when Merrill Swann can forget for a moment Grey Cup weeks, Rotary Conventions, and the multitude of other incomprehensible events that must all too often be endured in his chosen vocation.

The breasts of Dezura Shapiro come bouncing back through the main doors. His gaze and that of Mike Hatskill follow their jounce toward the elevators.

"Excuse me."

Merrill Swann stiffens as Mike Hatskill spins around, fussing into action. A small white-haired lady, as if from nowhere, is standing at the counter.

"So! On with it, Mr. Hatskill. Will confer later."

"Yes, sir."

Merrill Swann bends forward at the waist, smiling down to the lady. "Ma'am."

Then he scurries back toward his office, pausing only to remove a candy wrapper spied at the base of a plant and at the same time graciously delivering directions on the location of the gift shop to an elderly couple already near-buried under souvenirs.

* * *

Owen Coyle watches the fancy little guy with the white hanky, who seems to be someone in charge. Watches him as he heads back to the administrative offices, picking something out of a potted plant as he passes. He sees the desk clerk hand a little old lady something, then watches her toddle to the elevators on the heels of a big-chested woman dressed like a gypsy fortune-teller. He also notices the two uniformed and armed security guys who have just come down the escalator on his right from the second floor mezzanine.

He goes for a cigarette, has it out and in his mouth before he remembers. Old bad habits don't care too much for memory and he'll never get used to the anti-smoking laws. But everyone seems to have a gripe of some kind these days and no smoking in public places is one of the most popular, and why not, he figures. Probably makes a person feel somewhat superior and you don't have to go on protest marches or anything to support it. The perfect lazy man's cause.

He puts the cigarette back. He's been sitting here for fifteen minutes, already too long, but doesn't feel any real risk. There are so many people churning their way through the lobby, out from the elevators, up the escalators, across to the lounge, out to the street and in from the street. There's a definite air of wackiness, of barely contained mania. And a lot of white cowboy hats. A lot of red and white badges and ribbons with GO STAMPS GO! And a lot of red-faced pseudo-cowboy fat-cat nimrods.

Owen Coyle (stints in Kingston Pen, Drummond, and Stony Mountain Institution), who is 53 years old, 5 feet, 10 and 1/2 inches tall, and weighs 179 pounds, 3 ounces, gets to his feet in the main lobby of the Hyatt Regency Hotel on Burrard Street in Vancouver. He's a stocky ape-like man, broad across the shoulders, with short chunky legs that bow slightly beneath a sizeable belly. He moves slowly through the crowd, folding a newspaper under his arm, nameless and faceless, to all appearances just another visitor for Grey Cup week, even so far as to have a GO ARGOS button pinned to his coat. There is no evidence that there is anything missing about Owen Coyle, now making for the glass doors that lead out to the dull grey November day. Only Owen Coyle feels he is incomplete without the twelve gauge Mossberg "Slugster" slide action sawed-off he prefers to have tucked inside the right-hand side of his overcoat. Only Owen Coyle knows the Sterling .25 automatic with the four-and-a-half inch barrel is not now snug in its Holstein Grady shoulder holster under his left armpit. And only Owen Coyle is aware that he can't feel the pressure of the two-inch .38 Chief's Special automatic five-rounder taped to his right ankle, and that things will all be different the next time he visits the Hyatt Regency. What could be the same, however, he now knows, is that there could be at least two security guys in the lobby, maybe more, and if he had to know something about the next time he'd be here, that would be the something he'd want to know most.

8

Folk of Another World

.

JORGEN THRAPP SITS ALONE at a table in a darkened corner of the bar. A tiny crude rendition of the Nazca plateau Owl-man has been etched in the moisture on the side of his beer glass. He knows it was his finger that put it there but has no memory of guiding that finger. A thin sticky film of sweat coats his forehead. His hands tremble and he wonders what it all had been that he gulped down so recklessly only an hour or so ago while freaking out in the maintenance room. At first he was convinced they were uppers. So he took some downers. Then he changed his mind—they'd been downers. So he took some uppers. In the confusion, he had tossed a vial of Valium at poor Kristy, still standing tearfully in the doorway of the maintenance room, hoping to shut her up. And she immediately swallowed god knows how many, finally knocking over a mop stand and sinking to the floor. "I'm sorry, Jorgen. I just needed something."

"Get it together," he'd said, wishing someone was there to advise him the same way.

But Kristy was too far gone, too wacked-out by the responsibilities of being a stage manager, keeping happy the casts of three different opera productions. The problem of the moment, among the usual flotilla of others, is Heiner Blume, the male lead in *La Traviata*. The final straw had come for her that morning when Blume, who is 39 years old, 5 feet, 9 and 3/4 inches tall, and weighs 155 pounds, 4 ounces, requested, in a *not very nice way* according to Kristy, seedless oranges. It hadn't been difficult for Jorgen Thrapp to picture the asshole, standing on his tiptoes in the doorway of his dressing room, one hand impatiently stroking the purple and red silk cravat that he always wears to protect his throat, thin operatic nose held aloft.

"And I've never even heard of seedless oranges," Kristy had moaned.

And neither, in fact, had he, thinks Jorgen Thrapp, while steering her down the hallway away from the boiler room.

"I asked everyone," continued Kristy, "and everyone just looked at me funny. They looked *afraid*. I got so upset I became disoriented, I guess."

"Jesus, can't you just get him normal oranges?"

"It's the seeds. He's afraid they'll stick in his throat. You know how he is about his throat. It's insured for thousands. How he never sings in rehearsal, just speaks the lines to save his precious voice. And wears those dumb cravats all the time."

"It's okay. Remember last season when the broad in *Rigoletto* sent me out to get her tampons? These folk are not of this world, Kristy, I tell you. I'll find you some seedless oranges. Go tell Heiner Blowjob that."

And Kristy Kibsey was born again, smiling in gratitude as she staggered off to relay the good news to the blowjob Heiner Blume. And it was then that Jorgen Thrapp had headed for the bar, ostensibly looking for seedless oranges. He's never had any intention of actually looking for seedless oranges but has asked a few of the local patrons who have passed by his table. So far no one knows what he's talking about. And that's good. He'll have another drink and then make some dope deliveries. Ron Kanavrous doesn't need him until later that afternoon and, overall, not that much is different from any other working day.

But something is different.

He gets up to leave, pulling on his jacket and having a look around the bar. It's a number of blocks from the theatre and would be viewed as quite seedy by most of the theatre crowd. There's no chance of running into anyone from the theatre here. So why is he so nervous? Well, yeah, sure. All those pills he downed like an idiot in the maintenance room. But something more. It's that little talk with Kenny the printer.

That shit-ass Bernie the cop is supposed to be watching him. That was it. This was paranoia, man. Plain and simple.

He heads for the door, eyes catching the stocky form and broad shoulders of the guy just walking in. *Oh, christ,* thinks Jorgen Thrapp as he squeezes by Owen Coyle, who waits for him to pass, then takes a seat at the bar, Jorgen Thrapp hoping he can appear unconcerned, commanding himself to loosen the fuck up and walk normally. And once gaining the street, moving off quickly—*oh brother, did you check that guy—right out of the fucking cop fucking under-cover squad training fucking academy. The newspaper tucked under the arm, nice touch, pal. Real original. But I know what you're doing, fella. I know who you are. Bernie that shit-ass, I'm on to him. And you, I'm on to you too, my chubby little friend.*

A block down the street, he chances a look back, but the guy has stayed in the bar.

Look obvious, asshole, Jorgen Thrapp says to himself.

9

Lowdown Behaviour

HARRY PAZIK IS MOVING FAST in Room 414 of the Hyatt Regency. It's a search for the prized western bolo tie with the solid gold clasp fashioned in the two horns of a steer and the word 'Hank' engraved in the gold triangle between. And it's always irked him that his friends are only too quick to point out that 'Hank' is really short for Henry, not Harry. But he's always wanted a nickname of some kind, having known kids with the prestige of names like Terry 'Tank' Rothsteiner and Freddy 'Red-Bean' Barner. The 'Hank' had been an honest mistake on his part, but, the engraving done, there was no turning back and it had cost an effing fortune. He'd long ago accepted the error as a matter of course. Things happen. And he has worn it and will continue to wear it just as proudly as if he really had been named Henry instead of Harry.

He finds it curled neatly in an ashtray, and carries it delicately across the room between the tips of two fingers and lays it out by the bathroom sink where he rubs it down with a facecloth. The ugliness and guilt of awakening that morning with Dezura Shapiro still plagues him. Everything is an effort to make things appear normal, to erase the memory of the debauch altogether.

After Dezura Shapiro had finally left he'd lain in bed, the curtains still drawn as a defence against the harsh light of the new guilt-laden day. In fact, he'd lain there until two o'clock in the afternoon, when he at last managed to haul himself into the bathroom. It's unthinkable to look in the mirror; he applies himself to his business with eyes averted, tosses back some aspirin, and, with eyes still averted, plunges into the shower. The sting of the water helps, but doesn't quite succeed in convincing him that all that water is washing away the unsavoury slime he feels his entire body and being to be encased in. Such acts of infidelity and just plain drunken idiocy may be all right if done in the proper company, with good buddies from afar or complete strangers, but not in the great no-man's-land of family, relations, or the workplace. It was too much akin, he felt, to hunting without a valid hunting license. And worse, hunting a prey that is forever out of season.

The night that led up to the morning nightmare is nothing

more than a shady mish-mash of fragmented images featuring himself, Sid, Herb, and Teddy, Roger Shapiro and wife Dezura, and a few others, crawling the Vancouver West End bars and meeting on their way other Calgary supporters. Then back sometime to the hotel, yodelling (or something) through the lobby and falling down collectively in the elevator while making obscene gestures in the fish-eye mirrors. And at an unknown hour in Room 414, the beaded top of Dezura Shapiro suddenly seen floating by, yes, floating it was, high against the chintzy stucco ceiling and then falling, everyone else somehow disappearing, and Harry Pazik was swallowed up, swallowed up in the huge lust-mad drunken gulp of the moment.

Out from the shower, his eyes still averted from the mirror, his pale goose-bumped body wrapped in a towel, he trundles across the carpet to the night table where stands the bottle of Canadian Club.

He pours carefully.

The phone rings—a piercing, hellish sound. The towel drops and the whisky spills in a graceful arc from glass to belly, over and around and down, to envelope with an icy hand his unprotected balls. No time to even scream. No time to suck air. No time for nothing. *God in effing heaven, she knows! She knows everything I effing do!*

He lets the thing ring again, then picks it up.

"Main desk," a voice says. "Is this Mr. Pazik?"

Harry Pazik is silent. Why does he hesitate? "Yes, this is Mr. Pazik."

"Just a moment, please."

A pause and the voice of Celia Pazik crackles over the line, or maybe it's his mind that's crackling. "Harry? Harry, is that you?"

"Yes, Celia. It's me."

"Where have you been? I phoned earlier and a man answered who I thought was you but he—well, you told me to call today and I—"

"It must have been the wrong room or something, dear. I've been in my room all day."

"But I called again and the main desk put me through and there's been no answer and—"

"Oh, that must have been Herb, honey. He was here and used my phone to call home. I noticed just a moment ago that somehow he must've pulled the damn plug out of the wall."

"Oh. Well. You know Herb . . ."

"Yeah, I know."

"Would forget his head if it wasn't . . ."

"Yeah, that's Herb."

"So, how are you? Having a good time?"

"I'm fine. A little tired. Too much partying with the boys, I guess."

A weak chuckle, clears his throat. Allows him time for a swallow of whisky.

"You sound funny."

"I'm fine."

"Being good I hope."

"Oh, yes. Being good . . ." his fingers inadvertently crossing themselves. "Just been reading in my room today. How are the kids? Everything okay there?"

"Oh, yes, the kids are fine. You know, they didn't even notice you'd left until Sandy asked me yesterday where you were and I said your father's been gone already for three days. Isn't that crazy?"

Crazy, thinks Harry Pazik, to be so missed. Might as well lie about everything now. "Well, tell them I miss them too and I'll see you all sometime late Monday."

"Okay, dear—Oh! Are the Shapiros there?"

He straightens. Shoulders back, stomach in. A familiar contracting in his groin. Vulnerable, defenseless, naked.

"I only asked," she continues, "because Barbara said Roger was going to take Dezura. We all know she could care less about football. There's only one thing that woman is after, and she's not fussy either."

Thank you, Celia.

"The old snake in a rock pile, as Lois puts it, huh, Harry? Like you've said, honey, all Dezura Shapiro's got is big boobs, so big deal. And that's about it for her, eh, Harry?"

"Yes, Celia."

"That never bothered you about me did it, Harry? You've always said size doesn't matter—"

"I know, Celia. I know. Yes, the Shapiros are here. I had cocktails with them just last night. Dezura was as unbearable as ever."

"Oh, well. Watch her, Harry. She's poison. You know she's crazy."

"Out of her mind at best."

"And loose . . ."

"That too."

"She does drugs . . ."

"No scruples."

"She needs some kind of help, Harry."

"I believe that."

Silence. Harry drinks whisky, Celia exhales.

"Well, I guess that's all, hon. Enjoy yourself. I know you needed this break. The pressure was really getting to you here with the job and all and the market not being what it could, but it's just a slump. Things'll pick up. I know it."

"Yes, dear. It's good I can just be myself for a few days."

"That's good, dear."

"Good."

"Better go. Don't want a huge phone bill."

"Don't worry about that."

"See you Monday."

"Yup, Monday."

"Bye."

"Bye."

Tossing the phone aside, it's his turn to exhale, not aware he'd been holding his breath. But he does seem to be weathering the storm. Things might not be as bad as he'd been assuming. All might work out and his mistakes be buried under lies and deceit and be forgotten.

Happier now, and with renewed confidence, a naked and slightly blue Harry Pazik crosses to the bedside table and pours another drink, ignoring the towel on the floor. Now he lies full-length on the bed, glass resting on his belly. Sanity is returning. So far, so good. He worries too much, always nurturing doom. Better to exult. Exult in the unpredictability of life. It lends interest, excitement—life! The other would seem only to court boredom, becoming old and grey before one's time.

He closes his eyes.

The humidifier across the room hums, the faint sound of traffic from the street four floors down drifts through the slightly open window. These sounds aren't even recognizable for what they are but sound more like a calming deepsea wash, rising and breaking on some fictional shore, or a breeze rustling through a stand of white birch that sways above the banks of the Lower Bow River where he, Sid, and Herb had gone drift-boat fishing last summer, hauling in a catch of large browns and rainbows, frying them up that night over an open fire, lone hoot of a great horned owl and distant silhouette of a rare ferruginous hawk circling, the sun setting late over the low rise of the plains to the west as they lay stretched out, waiting for the dark, and for the sky to fill with a zillion stars.

He tenses his muscles. Lets them relax. Some kind of

relaxation exercise Celia does. The fire alarm blasts through the wall from the hallway, the glass toppling from his belly and an icy claw once more clutching at his balls as he finds himself exulting vehemently in the sudden unpredictability of life, and lets out a whoop while springing from the bed where he lands on his feet in front of the mirror, bug-eyed at his own reflection—an ape man, pale blue with red patches, expression of a deer in the headlights, one hand cupping his balls.

And which alarm was that? The thirteenth? Fourteenth? One-hundredth?

His reflection calms him. Or, rather, causes him to substitute one unsettling experience for another. A loose-fitting wrap of blotchy skin, clumps of dark hair on a pasty-white background. The flesh on his face hangs limp and drawn with dark stubble across his jaw. And his eyes—they are eyes, aren't they? He's seen something like them before, a photograph glanced in a *National Geographic* magazine down in the barber's a day or two ago, a shot of dense green foliage deep in the jungle, an exotic yellow-beaked black bird low on a tree, and just visible on the rocks below, fleeing the camera, two baboon's upheld red rear ends.

The fire alarm quits, and a naked Harry Pazik once more makes his way to the night table, thinking hardly once, let alone twice, about it and pours another drink. Sips this one standing, back to the mirror. Then pours another and walks cautiously to the bathroom where there are more mirrors.

Keeps the light off, his hand guiding gently and by habit, the twin-blade razor over his face. Combing his hair, the comb moving easily. A bit of aftershave, a roll of antiperspirant under the arms and now it's time to chance the light. And things don't look so bad this time, as a knock comes booming across the outer room and the voice of Roger Shapiro calls out faintly from the hall.

And in one effing second everything is awful again, a reflex to close and lock the bathroom door. And do what? Hide out? Great grieving shit—what lame-brain said they'd weathered the storm?

The knock comes again and now it's the voice that booms, Roger Shapiro wanting to know if he, Harry Pazik (weasel, slimeball, Judas), has seen Dezura. And a request to please open the door. Harry Pazik Junior in a fight-or-flight stance in the bathroom doorway, still not committed. Preparing his voice, getting ready to answer. Keep it calm, temperate (yeah, temperate)—ready for lies.

Then a new fear—had the unpredictable poisonous hippy Dezura Shapiro got everything? Had she removed every single personal belonging from Room 414 of the Hyatt Regency? The occupant hasn't really checked, has he? It's been enough just to get functional, let alone worry about covering his tracks.

Now, Harry Pazik, clean-shaven ape-man, is in flight mode from the bathroom doorway. Around the room, his eyes search for anything that might incriminate, lay bare,

bare as his jaybird self, the horrible truth. Spies the notice on the wall by the mirror and for a hare-brained moment wants desperately to place a call to the Long Branch Baptist Church. Why not, a prayer or two would be in order. Then sees it, peeking out from behind the six-drawer cherry laminate dresser. Some hastily far-flung black material. He crosses the room and holds aloft substantial black panties, the substantial black panties of Dezura Shapiro. Roger Shapiro at the door is asking once more, "Come on, let me in, Harry. Let me in, Harry, boy."

Harry boy, in the middle of the room, passes undies from hand to hand. When the next knock comes he takes three steps, firing them out the window, or almost, watches them fly bat-like through the air to stop against the closed glass and drop silently to the carpet. As he lunges after them, Roger Shapiro knocks again, his voice proclaiming at volume to anyone passing in the hall that it knows Harry Pazik's in there. Harry Pazik ignores the proclamation, a book, until now unnoticed, spied open on a chair. That too could only be Dezura's, *The Collected Works of John Donne*, open to the table of contents. And Harry Pazik reads, "Death be not proud"—(page 33). That's telling it like it is, and he grabs the book up. The window's out now, even if he opens it properly this time. Who knows what velocity a book would reach from the fourth floor. Glances over to the bed, once more down at the book. "Show me, dear Christ"—(page 32). That one is right on too. Goes for the bed, lifts the mattress where all the trouble had started in the first place. Then affords one last read before slamming the book shut and tucking it and the panties away. "I am a little world made cunningly"—(page 54).

Dezura's right. He should read more.

Now it's time to answer the door, remembering at the last minute to at least cover himself with a towel. Roger Shapiro stands there, a knuckled fist poised to pound once more.

"What the hell you been doing, Harry?"

"I was in the shower (then aware he's been dry for some time) —taking a shit."

"In the shower?"

"I mean—I had a shower and *then* I was taking a shit."

"Jesus, but that's real interesting, Harry. Have you seen Dezura? She stayed after we all left last night an' I haven't seen her this morning yet."

"She did? You haven't?"

"Yeah. Don't you remember?"

"No. I don't remember too much actually. I passed out. Just woke up awhile ago."

Roger Shapiro cranes his neck looking into the room, while Harry Pazik stares straight ahead out into the hallway under Roger Shapiro's raised armpit, catching a whiff of deodorant, aftershave, cigarettes.

"Kinda messed up your room, Harry. Quite a night, huh?"

"Sure was."

"I can't understand where she's gone."

"Maybe the shopping arcade downstairs."

"Yeah. Maybe. Well, I gotta find her. Catch you later."

"Yes. Later."

Roger Shapiro makes to go. Then turns back.

"Maybe she's in the lounge," he says.

"Could be," Harry says back.

"Or the restaurant . . ."

An uncomfortable silence, for Harry Pazik at least. He has nothing to say that wouldn't sound flat, forced, full of guilt and suspicion. They stare at each other, Roger Shapiro appearing for a moment to have drifted off. Then, as if suddenly cognizant of all the possibilities of where Dezura could be, he strides off down the hall.

* * *

But that was hours ago and Roger Shapiro hadn't returned with murder in his heart. Right now, in the early evening of the Saturday before the big game and after rinsing the ashes from the solid gold clasp of his prized western tie, the events of the day and night before seem far away. He's to meet Sid and the boys downstairs in the Gallery Bar, then march forth on the town. All is still in accordance with the big plan. No one is dead. The game's tomorrow. The bets are in. There are still seats on the forty-yard line and the Stamps will be champs.

Harry Pazik adjusts his tie, grabs his hat. A check of his wallet and a dab with a towel on his boots and he closes the door of Room 414 of the Hyatt Regency, while about eight blocks away, in accordance with their own laws of infidelity and just plain low-down behaviour, Calgary linebacker Mad Joe Mezzaroba and defensive tackle Bobby Mashtaler stifle giggles as they sneak down the fire stairs of the Bayshore Inn, intent on a night on the town themselves, an intent that would never be in accordance with the wishes of coach Willy Brisco, who lies propped up in his hotel bed watching game tapes and drafting ideas and stratagem to win that fucking game tomorrow.

10

Higher Insidious Powers

JORGEN THRAPP EMBRACES his Saturday in a blind tableau of survival: tapping feet, wringing hands, upper body jerking at every little sound and movement. There are the after-affects of the various unknown drugs taken the day before, but there are other things too. Opening night jitters are peaking for cast and crew, none of whom seem to think they're anywhere near ready to put on an opera. And Kristy Kibsey may well just off herself after learning that Jorgen Thrapp could not locate any seedless oranges for the dipshit Heiner Blume. Thankfully, Ron Kanavrous asks little of him, only to retrieve his tuxedo from the rental agency and take his car in for servicing. That, and to have two ciabatta veggie wraps (plenty of salt) and the customary Thermos of Johnny Walker Black (mixed three parts whisky to one part water) ready and available for the dress rehearsal in the afternoon where they sit now, in the eighth row of the darkened theatre. Jorgen Thrapp drifts between a dozy delerium and the gut-stabbing horrors of drug withdrawal. The juxtaposition of lighting and certain pieces of the set have somehow combined to render an unfortunate shadow across the stage backdrop that resembles to a T a slightly oblong Owlman. Sinister omen or benevolent spirit, he doesn't know, and replies to Ron Kanavrous's questions in monosyllables whenever possible, finding complete sentences just too much effort.

The Fat Man and the assistant director sit a few seats over in the same row, issuing directions to those onstage. Occasionally, Jorgen Thrapp makes dashes to the lobby to call Kenny the printer, cajoling, threatening, and pleading to ensure the numbers sheets will be ready by at least five that afternoon. And Ron Kanavrous keeps up an almost constant dialogue into his headset to the lighting operator ensconsed in the black operations booth high in the darkness at the back of the theatre. More red here. Less blue there. More intensity, less intensity. Colours blend and undulate across the stage. Periodically, Jorgen Thrapp glimpses a multi-coloured Kristy Kibsey, appearing a little lost, clipboard in hand, and wandering the shadows in the wings. So nothing is helped when the Fat Man shouts "No! No!" and gets to his feet to make his trek down to the stage. Jorgen Thrapp and Ron Kanavrous climb over their seats into the row behind to let him by and from there Jorgen Thrapp watches as the Fat Man climbs onto the stage only to teeter on the edge of the orchestra pit, then fall forward with a grunt and disappear from sight. Everyone rushes to the mouth of the pit, Ron Kanavrous pulling off his headset and running down the aisle. Jorgen Thrapp does some rushing of his own too, mostly internal, and ends up wandering the corridors of the theatre, occasionally leaping from what appear to be naked men and women lurking in the doorways and around corners. He makes for the common room where he gulps coffee, watching as the walls steadily close in.

Fatigue, opening night jitters, he tells himself. And the return of the Owl-man. But the level of paranoia and general feelings of doom seem greater than that. And it's not so much to do with fat men toppling into orchestra pits. That does screw things up, true, but his thoughts keep returning to Kenny the printer and Bernie the shit-ass. Getting busted no longer seems improbable, something to laugh off. It seems almost inevitable the way things are going. Some over-zealous reporter would no doubt publish government figures of how much it costs to keep a single prisoner behind bars for one year, with his, Jorgen Thrapp's, mugshot on the front page. This, in turn, would enrage the public who would want him got rid of, snuffed out to save those pennies. There are higher insidious powers at work in the universe, which every gambler, criminal, and he himself knows, powers that can take the odds and doctor them any which way to suit some cosmic plan of justice, moving the stars just so and dumping the shit on those chosen.

So it is that having survived the day, that night he finds himself hunkered down in Ron Kanavrous's office under cover of darkness, seeking shelter and anonymity while rummaging through the drawers behind the desk and drunkenly scribbling notes.

Dear Ron,
Thanks for the use of the couch and the bottle one has found, as one sleeps the sleep nightmares are made of.

At midnight, as Jorgen Thrapp sleeps the sleep, Harry Pazik takes a left at one corner and a right at the next. Then another right. And a left. He crosses the street to that side, then back to this side. And at last trips up on the curb, sprawling onto the sidewalk.

He lies there, winded. Incredulous at his inability to breathe. Unable to see, Stetson down over his eyes, chin compacting against the pavement under the glare of the street lights. And scrawled in red lipstick across the back of his hat, the words:

And as one falls, two others rise. Roger Shapiro and Ralph Hogg get up from their chairs on the balcony of Suite 615 of the Hyatt Regency on Burrard Street, overlooking the Melville Street entrance. Ralph Hogg has interrupted their game to voice alarm, hoisting the bottle of Canadian Club and pointing to the inch or so of whisky left. Roger Shapiro reassures him by delivering the information that another two bottles sit just inside the room behind the closet door and they can get them any time they want to. Placated, Ralph Hogg sits back down and resumes the game.

"Have we said *dick* yet?"

"Think so."

"Bone. Prick. *Big Balogne?*"

"Big Balownee . . ." says Roger Shapiro, his voice trailing off as he peers out over the railing to the street below.

"Balowneee . . . balowneeeee—"

He grasps the railing. A faint booming, with a beat, pounds up through the night air from somewhere below. Butt Ugly is giving it their all from the Plaza Ballroom.

Ralph Hogg ponders aloud. "Dink. Waldo. Wang Dang Doodle . . ."

Roger Shapiro leans dangerously out, releasing a cry. "HEY PAZIK! YOU SCUMMY BASTARD! YOU BEEN FUCKING MY WIFE!"

Harry Pazik has emerged from the underground station of the SkyTrain on the other side of Melville Street. And now struggles up the station stairway, intent only on reaching

Room 414 of the Hyatt Regency after another night of Grey
Cup festivities. He'd somehow become separated from Sid
and Herb but remembers vaguely he'd been befriended by a
group of high-spirited, and, it turned out, quite cordial
Toronto fans. They'd all been quite neighbourly and he'd
obliged them in a true sporting way by allowing his hat to
make the rounds at the table. Upon gaining street-level, he
can hear the faint boom and crash of drums and bass, Christ
Church Cathedral lit up off to his left, across Burrard, a
viable clue to his whereabouts. The Hyatt should be dead
ahead, and he makes for a hotel-looking lighted doorway. He
crosses Melville Street and steadies himself upon gaining
the sidewalk on the other side. An empty whisky bottle
smashes on the sidewalk to his right, a hotel lamp to his left.
He turns in a circle, confused by the sudden barrage—*What,
dear Celia, is happening?*—then pushes on. Just a few more
steps. One floor up, in the Plaza Ballroom, Butt Ugly is beating its way through "No More To Say," a crowd favourite.
Lead guitarist, Dingo, is leaping like a man possessed to the
encouragement of the crowd, when he catches a foot in a
tangle of cables by the edge of the stage at the height of an
ear-piercing E7 chord, requiring him to perform an
impromptu pirouette in a hopeless attempt to save himself,
but he fails, taking half the sound equipment and a Coke
bottle full of rum and the same down onto the floor. There
the whole heap explodes in a spray of liquid, smoke, and
sparks and the fire alarm—for the first time that week—at

last takes up its cry for the legitimate reason it was originally installed.

Lights flicker and sporadically go out in the hotel and Harry Pazik, still reeling under the street lights, attempts to advance once more. A voice calls his name and something else he's unable to make out as a mattress drops out of the murky black above, landing in front of him, bouncing, rising once and then coming down right across the golden hooves of his prized western tie.

And he is again sprawled on the pavement, held down by an unseen weight. He glimpses his white Stetson rolling along the sidewalk as the mattress holds him to the pavement, the Stetson twirling along on its brim like a lost hubcap to the hotel steps where it stops. A well-lit vision of a hotel employee on a smoke break pauses, then steps down and bends over. About to retrieve the hat, *good lad, he'll return it*, though the employee only holds the hat, staring at it, appearing thoughtful, then amused, the image breaking up as Harry Pazik sighs, laments the callous hearts of others, and passes out.

Assorted Unknown Pills

11

Buddies

I, HARRY PAZIK, THINKS Harry Pazik, am in some kind of trouble. *I've just been sitting in my ranch-style game room watching the game, but not with the boys.* On the faux leather couch sit the Ice Hog family, mascots from Ottawa's Winterlude Festival (attended many times throughout his youth): big black noses, huge front teeth that look filed, alleged magical furry little creatures that crossed the ice bridge over the Bering Strait thousands of years ago, so the brochures say, now sitting in the game room sipping beer and making all kinds of obnoxious sounds while one of them tosses a beer can, dislodging a revered framed original photograph of the 1928 Calgary Tigers football team that clatters to the floor amidst the cigar butts strewn at their feet. Then a sudden change of venue, a tiny-tot Harry Pazik

Junior skating, unsteady child muscles trying to learn the ropes of coordinating blades of sharpened steel across the rough frozen surface of the Rideau Canal, tiny legs burning, snot iced along a tiny blue upper lip. And scenes spinning by of some best-forgotten high school traumas, then one of white-water rafting down the Kananaskis with Celia and the kids, on their faces expressions of joy or terror of the new life in the West; it's impossible to tell. And it does hurt most above and behind the eyes. A good solid wall of pain in his chest and a fine old church of heaven that Christ Church Cathedral is—a sign remembered, glimpsed just before the pain—*The Sermon for Today: Surviving Life.* God does talk to people, he guesses. And flying carpets—no, mattresses. Down from the sky. And Celia—no, there's no Celia. A grey membrane sac, that's the brain. Not pretty. Bounced around a bit in there. And sidetable lamps and other hotel things coming down from out of the night sky. A voice—the voice of Ralph Hogg—the cartoon *boing!* of bedsprings . . . um . . . the sparkle of shattered glass. And Ralph asking if he's okay. Up from where the hotel things came down from. Nice guy, that Ralph, even after what's been done to his buddy. A hotel employee illuminated under the lights, coming over, and asking kindly as to his welfare. Holding his white cowboy hat in long fingers as a small red and white blur spins through the night air, it too coming down to bounce once off his head and into the night again, and spinning the words: GO STAMPS GO.

He sits up, calling out from the pain.

A strange bed—oh, no, not another indiscretion—another fleshy cannon somewhere aimed at the heavens, hot-air balloons. No, a hospital room this time. And alone, thank god. White plastic bracelet around the wrist with his name, a room number and blurry clues written beneath that. And don't worry, Celia, it's okay. Your guy has been checked into somewhere. No plush carpets, no complimentary bar—*and nobody else.* Hold it, the door in the wall is opening. Don't remember calling room service. A woman in white with a sympathetic smile, exuding safety, protection. On a stainless steel tray he spies some unfamiliar gadgets, but no cocktails. And a voice, practiced, measured.

"Now, now. You've had quite a knock, Mr. Pazik. Please lie back down."

He glances around the room for the oversized Ice Hog family on a bedside vigil, but there's no sign of them and he sinks back onto the pillows. The voice again, practiced, measured. "How are you feeling?"

"I don't know. Where am I?"

"You're in the hospital, Mr. Pazik. St. Paul's. I'm Nurse Worner. You've had an accident." The stainless steel tray plunks down.

"Ow. Nurse, pain . . . everywhere."

"You'll be fine, Mr Pazik. A slight concussion. A fractured rib."

"Fractured rib, Nurse? Concussion?"

"Now, now, Mr Pazik. It's quite all right. A little uncomfortable, but you're going to be okay. Please lie back."

"But, where—"

"Ward 3, Mr. Pazik. You're on Ward 3 . . ."

"The hospital, yes?"

"Yes, Mr. Pazik. Relax, please. You're going to be fine."

"I don't remember . . ." He lies still, curling his toes.

"A mattress I believe it was, Mr. Pazik."

"A mattress, Nurse Worner?"

"Yes, a mattress, Mr. Pazik. You were hit by a mattress."

"How—"

"Someone got carried away."

"Carried away. I'll say—what are you doing?"

"Just taking your blood pressure, Mr. Pazik. Lie still, please."

"I was at the hotel . . ."

"That's right. You do remember something."

"The hotel . . . what time is it?"

"Ten-forty-five. Or close to."

"But *when* nurse. WHEN!"

Nurse Worner pulls back, startled. "Why, it's Sunday, Mr. Pazik. Sunday morning. You were brought in last night. Well, early this morning to be exact."

A muted cry. "My god, Nurse Worner. What is happening to me?"

"Please, Mr. Pazik. You're going to be all right. You must take it easy." She pats his arm, pumping air into the rubber bulb. The dial needle moves, then stops. She leans over. "Ah, that's good, Mr. Pazik. Very good."

"What's good, Nurse. I have to get out of here. I've come a long way for this and now I'm going to miss it!"

"You're going to have to rest, Mr. Pazik. I'll fetch the doctor and we'll give you something more for the pain. You're still in somewhat critical condition. With injuries to the head there can be complications. Oh, and your friends came by and left this for you. Said they couldn't wait around. I'll be back shortly."

She pulls out a piece of paper, and Harry Pazik fumbles for it. Oh, yes, goody gumdrops. Words of comfort from friends, to let him know all is well. He shouldn't have panicked, acted the ass in front of Nurse Worner. It would be wise to keep on her good side. Nurse Worner closes the door.

He reads the note:

Dear Harry stayed as long as we could
you're going to be okay so we had to get
going will see you later sorry buddy you
have to miss the game your pal Herb and all.

*   *   *

Someone else is also coming to in a confused state in a strange place. Jorgen Thrapp does so on the couch in Ron

Kanavrous's office, awakening just as he's being strapped into the chair in the glass cubicle, sporting a jailhouse tattoo of the Owl-man on his left forearm. Mom, Dad, Gramps, and Grams are there, seated on the other side of the glass as the cyanide begins mixing with the sulphuric acid. No one had told him it was a capital offense to run numbers. And Kenny the printer is there too, his arm around Bernie the shit-ass. Heiner Blume is nodding in solemn agreement with the verdict from the shadows, eating an orange with seeds the size of grapefruits, as Ron Kanavrous lurks somewhere out of sight, whistling to himself and adjusting the lights in the cubicle while eating some concoction that still has the fins on it.

He throws the blanket aside and staggers off the couch, shaking off the dream. The feet aren't working too well, the legs rubbery. A few shaky steps to the door where he thrusts his head into the hallway. The coast looks clear. He moves hesitantly along the hall, clothes damp against his skin. Finds the washroom and puts his weight against the door. Inside, he splashes cold water over his face. Moving then to take a pee, wavering slightly over the urinal. He's careful of the zipper coming up, can't trust the motor reflexes. And what was Kenny the printer doing there, at his execution, dream or not? And he didn't look too concerned either. Nor did the folks for that matter. Back to the sink, more cold water on his face, running a wet comb through his hair. Some sharp slaps from his palms across stubbled cheeks, a coughing fit that borders on choking and he approaches the door to leave, not knowing why he's walking on tip-toes. Head pokes into the hallway, wiping away tears from the coughing fit. Once again the coast is clear but he's still afraid the place may well come to life with a thousand disparaging faces at any moment, unhappy to see him at this or any other time. It's just the withdrawal, he tells himself. And the hangover. And the paranoia. It's early and the city still sleeps; all is well. He straightens his shoulders and makes for the maintenance room, while a mile and a half away, not sleeping at all, well over ten thousand people are wide awake and crowding the downtown streets, not the least of whom is Mayor Dusty Moons. The Mayor sits curled in the seat of a silver Bentley Arnage Drophead Coupe convertible waiting impatiently for the start of the Grey Cup Parade, and is, in his own words, "freezing his black ass off."

12

Artistic Types

ARMAND CUVALLO (stints in Collins Bay Institution and Beaver Creek) not so much "spends" his Saturday as endures it, holed up in the small housekeeping room just off Commercial Drive in Vancouver's East End. Armand Cuvallo of faded indigo and blue-green plaid cotton shirts and well-worn flat-front belted dress pants of polyester-viscose (owns two pairs: one in olive green, another in taupe). One pair of stone-grey no-name sneakers from the Sally Ann always laced tight, keep feet secure and protected and are removed only for sleeping. An antiquated AM/FM clock radio on the windowsill plays tinny-sounding country music as he sips vodka from a bottle. He intersperses the reading of a cheap pocket mystery with arbitrary sections of the newspaper or one of the seven or so magazines scattered about the room. A 747 has crashed in Korea. A typhoon has ripped up Guangdong province in China. Everything's changing all the time and at the same time, well, staying the same. To Armand Cuvallo, the news of the world only helps to validate what he's known all along since he was a skinny boy growing up in Thunder Bay, Ontario, and that's that the world's a very scary and dangerous place to be at any time. And when not reading, he may stare out the window, or just shut his eyes, yellowed fingers raising a cigarette to his lips. He's still not fully recovered from the last attack and the vodka doesn't seem to be helping.

He'd been out earlier in the day and that was enough. Thought to get something to eat, kill some time and get some air. Easy enough. He was staring in a gift-shop window up The Drive at plaster of Paris busts of dogs in humorous poses, wearing hats and smoking cigars, when the attack came, the first in months, and it took him by surprise. He'd thought maybe they'd gone, like forever. But then again, Armand Cuvallo can't really believe that anything bad is ever gone forever. The dizziness, sounds, and smells are suddenly exaggerated to a stupid degree and he's panicking and trying to head back up the street to his room—stopping and leaning up against a storefront window. Closing his eyes, everything starting to swirl now, sounds amplified: voices from people passing. Traffic. One humdinger of a screech from some craphead on the road quite nearby laying a strip of rubber. And when he opens his eyes again, it's to see his own reflection, terrified and staring back at him from a shop window. A round man wielding a meat cleaver that rises and seems to slice downward right through his skull. It's a moment before he realizes the man is inside the store, barely visible behind his reflection, and is just chopping meat behind the counter. He somehow manages to get his ass moving again up the sidewalk, grabbing a sandwich, milk, and cigarettes in a corner store on the way back. Coins scatter over the counter when he's paying and run like angry little buzz-saws along the floor. Lunges for the door, "Watchitfella!" as he steps on some guy's toes, outside the sidewalk reeling under him, sky rigid above like something long and flat and solid and appearing to descend slowly and he sees himself four years, four months, and four days old, in formal dress and ready to recite his first verse of the Koran. His father is stern. And proud. The verse is written in honey on a slate and once he gets the recitation right, the honey is dissolved in water. He is told to drink the water. He is told to drink the holy words.

In the room, he reaches for the vodka and some pills. The tinny music plays. He lies out on his back across the scattered magazines and newspapers on the floor, a cold wet cloth over his face, arms splayed, like a man crucified or about to be pulled in quarters. If the pills and vodka work, if he can just remember how the honey words tasted, maybe he can get some sleep.

He awakes early Sunday morning, hauling his tired body to the tiny basin clinging precariously to the wall. A long green stain runs down into the drain, residue of other rubbed and wasted faces. He washes and shaves. He hadn't undressed, except for the stone-grey no-name sneakers, and these he fishes out from under the bed. Then he drags out a suitcase and plops it on top of the magazines and newspapers. Flicks it open and lifts out the 12-gauge Browning BPS pump sawed-off and a pistol, the Smith & Wesson .38 four-inch Special. Inspects the shotgun affectionately. The shortened barrel increases the shot spread to four feet at ten yards and jacks the power by enough to blow an oak door off its hinges at six. It's good that way; it can hit anything that scares you. He feels better.

A few hours later it's nestled snugly along his right side under the knee-length raincoat. The Smith & Wesson, the ace in the hole, is tucked into its holster under his left arm. The breeze is stiff and cold off the harbour, and he and Owen Coyle and Sam Labovic are looking across the water from the plaza at the foot of Granville Street to the mountains on the North Shore. The SeaBus ferry approaches across wind-blown water. Owen Coyle is smiling, feeling complete at last with the Mossberg "Slugster" riding comfortably in its sling up his left side under his coat. The Sterling .25 automatic makes a small lump where it hangs under his arm, and the little .38 Chief's Special applies pressure where it's wrapped securely around his right ankle, under his pant leg.

And Sam Labovic, travelling the lightest of the three, feels quite content with the Commander Colt .45 stuffed into his inside coat pocket. All three stand huddled against the harbour-side railing, collars up, hands shoved deep in pockets or one occasionally guiding a cigarette to dry cold lips. A few gulls hover on the air above, expertly staying in the same spot while buffeted by the wind. Sam Labovic watches them while listening to Armand Cuvallo. When Cuvallo finishes, he asks him, "Was it bad?"

"No, not so bad," says Armand Cuvallo.

"That's still not so good."

"It's been worse. Much worse."

Sam Labovic turns, his eyes holding Armand Cuvallo's. Then turns to Owen Coyle. "Armand's agaro—agorasome-thing . . ."

"Agoraphobic," says Armand Cuvallo.

"That so?" says Owen Coyle. He has his shoulders hunched to his ears and bounces on the spot from foot to foot. "Well, shit."

"So. What do you think," says Sam Labovic.

"It'll be okay. I'm all right," says Cuvallo, staring straight ahead.

"You sure?"

"Yeah, I'm sure."

"Don't want any fucking around."

"No fucking around. I'm okay. Tired of waiting, that's all."

"We just don't need any fucking around."

"Don't worry about the fucking around. Won't be any fucking around."

"Better fucking not be."

"Fuck the fucking around," says Owen Coyle. "What about Martin?"

"Talked to him Thursday morning," says Sam Labovic, "just before his rehearsal. Everything's set."

"Better fucking be."

"Don't you start."

"Well, if you want fucking around, ask Martin."

"He'll come through."

"All artistic types fuck around. Especially musicians."

"Marty'll do fine. Don't worry about it."

The gulls veer off to the right, over the water, then fall back again and plummet shrieking to the tracks that run immediately below. Sam Labovic watches their flight, thinks of the eagles he'd been told to pay attention to while working the logging camps. Thoughts of the logging camps threaten to remind him of more than he cares to remember at this time, so he snaps his eyes away.

Owen Coyle is talking. ". . . and so maybe you can re-convince me on all this, like, isn't a bank a more lucrative option than a hotel for all intents and purposes in a case like this?"

Sam Labovic inhales, exhales towards the mountains. "Okay. Banks are, in the normal course of things, more lucrative as you say. And they're also fifty to a hundred times more jacked up security-wise too. High risk. According to Martin, we're unlikely to be disappointed with the hotel score although most will probably be stones, not cash. But that's okay, even better. More worth for the weight. No idea of how much cash there may be, if any."

Owen Coyle bounces on his feet. "Am I re-convinced?"

"Dunno. Are you? Let me know."

All three men are silent a moment. A SeaBus ferry blows its whistle faintly from the far shore.

"So here it is," says Sam Labovic, "I know you two guys like the hardware, you're probably packing a ton of iron right now. You know I don't, so maybe you guys could knock it down to one piece apiece, you know what I mean? Also, back in the car I got these so-called "transition" out-doorsy jackets or some fucking thing covered in logos, stripes, and general bright-coloured horseshit all around. Ugly stuff. We wear these in and out. Easy for people to remember and hopefully describe. Once in the car, we ditch 'em and get back into our usual drab and uninspired garb."

Armand Cuvallo stands motionless with his face to the wind, his thoughts his own. Owen Coyle laughs, turns his back to the breeze to light another cigarette. "What time's the game start, anyway?"

"Two o'clock, I think," says Sam, again watching the gulls that are scavenging along the tracks below.

"Now, sports events, gentlemen," says Owen Coyle.

"You want fucking around, there's your fucking around. This place is a madhouse. Like the whole city's pulling its wire. At least nobody'll be paying attention. I prefer a quiet time myself, something with a little deeper meaning, you know. I'm getting too old for anything that smacks of meatball commercialized bullshit."

Sam Labovic snorts. "Yeah, well, remember. No meatball commercialized bullshit shooting if you can help it. Scary. That's all it's supposed to be, just *scary*."

"Ya, Boss," says Owen Coyle. "I will shoot only ceilings or floors, *not* the walls."

Outdoorsy Jacket

"You're one fine meatball commercialized bullshit motherfucker of a gentleman, Mr. Coyle," says Sam Labovic.

"Do my best," says Owen Coyle.

The SeaBus ferry noses into its slip below them, but the angle's a little off and it bumps the slip. Someone can be heard yelling something and Owen Coyle glances down, then looks triumphantly at Sam Labovic. Sam Labovic watches the gulls launch themselves from where they've wandered up the tracks. They catch an updraft and soar out and away over the harbour.

"See this? Captain's giving them shit," shouts Owen Coyle. "The whole crew, like the whole bloody town, isn't paying attention. Too busy. Too busy pulling their goddamn wires!"

13

The Maimed and Dying

IT'S NOT WITHOUT DIFFICULTY that Harry Pazik makes his way through the main admitting lobby of the hospital, head throbbing, his left leg jack-knifing into his abdomen with each spasm of pain that rifles down from his ribcage. The idea to leave the hospital is not premeditated, but just rears up from the constant pain and general distress of the moment, plus the horrible meaning of the note from Herb and the boys. All that mixed with some inducement, he doesn't doubt, from the ideology absorbed and retained while growing up under the heavy eye of Harry Pazik Senior, and that is: even when one may not at such moments be clear on much, something, after all, has to be done to at least suggest a modicum of control and competence in the participant. And a short meeting with the doctor hadn't helped things, with Harry slipping in and out of cognitive memory of recent events, and, for that matter, of larger segments of his entire life, lying with head wrapped in bandages and sunk heavily into the pillow as the doctor stood above him, his slightly (they looked to Harry) purplish lips moving at the bottom of his narrow face, saying things like, "A blow like this . . . twisting of the brain structures and blood vessels . . . breakdown of the normal flow of messages within the brain . . ."— a reference then to a *Dora*, or *Doowa*, or something—outer covering of the brain, or was it the armpit? And Harry laid out and submissive under the hospital blankets, nodding at the purplish lips as they fluttered up and down, saliva seen reflecting off them every once in a while, and so forthcoming with information, a foreboding list of cautions: *concussion, loss of memory, irrational behaviour.*

And most of this was heard, maybe acknowledged, then promptly forgotten again, the purplish lips finally smacking together twice with authority and remaining still a moment, then saying the words, "Well, then," and they were gone as mysteriously as they'd appeared. And Harry Pazik then trying to put the lie to all the doctor's ranting (he was ranting, wasn't he?) pulling up some quite valid and even clear memories to prove him wrong. For instance, he knows damn well he lives in Calgary, a *ranch* house—well, not a ranch house on a ranch, but . . . he has a wife and two—maybe three—kids. And a dog, well, maybe the neighbour's. And there's a lodgepole pine in the backyard, or was that the childhood home back in Ottawa? No. That was an elm. With a rope swing. Of course, he can remember it all.

And Hank is a derivative of Henry, not Harry. But what Harry Pazik doesn't know is that he'll have a harder time remembering the next twenty-four hours than anything in the distant past, as in the hours to come, a small part of his brain will swell, infinitesimally, but enough to cause short-term memory loss on and off, much like the nightlight in his childhood room fashioned in the head of Disney's Goofy that flickered through the long winter nights but a snow-ball's throw from the icy Gatineau River. And, (still putting the lie to the doctor) there's a stone goldfish pond, iced over, never any goldfish anyway, too much upkeep, and this image doesn't even warrant memory, just logic, for who living on the Great Plains in the foothills of the effing Rockies would have such an item in their backyard in the first place? So that was definitely a memory of childhood in Ottawa and not a memory of—um, that other city where one lives on the Prairies.

And then he manoeuvres himself out of the hospital bed before the return of Nurse Worner, stifling moans while struggling into his clothes and balancing precariously on one leg, then the other, leaning against the effing closet door that keeps swinging shut. And once out in the hall of Ward 3, as the blazing fluorescent lights and lack of concealment increase his agitation and feed his panic, he manages, with a heroic effort, to pass the nurses' station with a minimum of grunts and groans, teeth gritted in what he hopes will pass as a smile. His Stetson covers the bandages around his head for the most part and luckily no one looks up. At the elevator, he manages another frightening smile at a passing nurse who smiles back, and he holds strong a jaw-locked smile until the elevator doors close and he's able to sag against the elevator wall and let go a wail. He wails a couple more times on the ride down, safe within the soundproof walls of the elevator. At the second floor the doors slide open, and a small army of white uniforms enter. He stays wedged near the doors, allowing the white wave to press by to the rear. Someone's laughing and he's sure it's at him. He pays no attention, face fixed to the front.

A not-good moment comes when the doors open on the main floor and his legs falter in the doorway, feeling the crowd surging forward from behind. Another heroic and painful effort needed to manage a pivot out of the elevator, pressing his body to the wall while grabbing for stability a chrome ashtray secured there (installed, no doubt, some time before the no-smoking laws), and clinging there a moment, readying himself for the open terrain of the admitting lobby ahead. And just to get this far has been no mean feat, by god, he never knew he had it in him. And concussion be damned, he remembers with no problem the seats on the forty-yard line, a room at the Hyatt something Hotel, somewhere, and the big game, the Grey or Pewter Cup, no problem. That's where he has to be, to get to. That's what it's all about.

Now he gauges the open terrain of the admitting area ahead of him, gathering strength. Then pushes off into the expanse, free-wheeling, like he's in a free-fall of sorts, not vertically but horizontally. He reassures himself that no one expects people in a hospital to walk normally, how could they with all the maimed and dying? He allows himself a heavy (and in his condition, necessary) limp and makes for the phones by the main doors. It all seems tediously slow but in fact he makes good time once out on the floor. People seem only too eager to get out of his way. He gets a jolt of confidence when an elderly man still in his pajamas and on crutches wipes out on a standing plant, old man and crutches skidding to the floor. Hospital staff and others rush to administer aid. A good diversion if Nurse Worner or others are on the move, tracking him down. He reaches the phones and grabs the taxi-direct line, hoarse croak into the receiver, then shuffles outside to wait. And takes a nervous glance or two over his shoulder, fearing the sight of Nurse Worner, pissed and coming out the doors with two, maybe three male nurses in tow to take him, by force if necessary, back to his room.

No, the decision to leave the hospital had not been pre-meditated, but now, almost free and feeling more and more like a man with a mission, he knows it's the only thing to do. He's come to see, be part of, *ingest* a national sports celebration—not watch it on a four-inch screen from an adjustable bed surrounded by the sick and infirm. There is a seat on the forty-yard line for his unapologetic ass only and a room on the fourth floor of a downtown hotel that cost dearly, so much so that he may have to wait another year to buy that new set of golf clubs he's been wanting. And he was simply *meant* to be there, with friends, guzzling beer and going crazy or doing whatever the hell you were supposed to do at a big game. Nurse Worner had been kind and sympathetic, but still hadn't volunteered to call him a taxi. No, there's no inner searching necessary here. He has to go. He has to.

He looks frantically up and down the outside parkway for sign of a cab. A spasm of pain, his left leg jack-knifing. Good god, there should be awards, recognition given to fans that place loyalty to their team before their own health and well-being. A cab is pulling up and he dives forward, unmindful of his condition. Grabs the door handle and wrenches said door open, letting go a cry of agony as his left leg jack-knifes once more into his abdomen, forcing him to spin involuntarily. He collapses on his side across the back seat of the cab, a sharp expulsion of air, the driver turning with a look of concern, and Harry flashing a reassuring lock-jawed smile from the prone position while struggling to hook the toe of his Tony Lama cowboy boot into the inside door handle and pull the effing door shut.

"You okay, sir?"

"I'm fine! Fine. I'll just stay this way until we get there. Good for my back. The Hyatt whatsit, on the double.

Burrard Street, I think. And for god's sake, turn on the radio!"

*   *   *

Down on the playing field of BC Place, Mayor Dusty Moons finishes his Grey Cup speech and approaches the ball for the ceremonial kickoff. His patent-leather shoes slide treacherously over the AstroTurf; he takes quick dancing steps. His toe connects and the ball piddles off to the right for a few yards where it spins, falters, and lies still. The crowd erupts in a deafening roar, fortified by everything from stadium beers to vodka-spiked Thermoses. It's impossible for Dusty Moons to tell if it's a good-natured cheer of enthusiasm or a humiliating guffaw for such a lame kick. He adjusts his collar and with the other dignitaries makes his way off the field, careful to keep his eyes off the stands.

"Nice try, sir."

"Thank you, Mr. Dwyer."

"Anyone could have had trouble in those shoes, sir."

"That's what I was thinking, Mr. Dwyer."

"Maybe should've put on those complimentary cleats, sir."

"I don't think so, Mr. Dwyer."

"Of course not, sir. Well, it's almost over."

"Oh, no, Mr. Dwyer. That I don't believe. Don't believe it for a minute."

14

Spastics

MIKE HATSKILL STARES first into the cold grey eyes of Owen Coyle and then into the black hole of the muzzle of the Mossberg Slugster slide-action sawed-off poking out from the guy's multi-striped and gaudy-coloured outdoorsy looking jacket. His stomach rises, then sinks, then curls into a tight little ball that seems to suck all the blood up from his toes and down from his face to pool and constrict in his chest. Sam Labovic, standing beside Owen Coyle in his own multi-striped and equally gaudy-coloured outdoorsy looking jacket, repeats the instructions again.

"Call the manager. NOW!"

Mike Hatskill jerks his eyes from the muzzle of the Mossberg to the guy who just spoke—a deadpan serious expression on this one too, means business, eyes like dark glass. He picks up the phone, hands beginning to shake as he punches the dial button once. His tongue comes out to lick his lips. The most bizarre thing is that nothing else in the lobby has changed. People are still going about their business, shuffling by, oblivious to the drama unfolding at the main desk, the drama fucking unfolding to him, and him alone. The tongue comes out again. A prickly heat ascends his neck invading his scalp. He speaks into the phone. "Mr. Swann. Hatskill here. Would you have a moment, please?"

*   *   *

Armand Cuvallo sits tensed in a chair by the main doors, eyeing the two uniformed and armed security guys who have just come down one of the escalators from the mezzanine floor. They step off to the side at the bottom and remain there against the wall, idly surveying the lobby and occasionally exchanging conversation. The door to the administrative offices opens down the far wall to his left and he watches the well-dressed jaunty little guy hurriedly cross the lobby carpet to the front desk. He sees the desk clerk lean forward and say something and watches as the jaunty little guy's expression changes. It looks like the guy's going to take a piss or something as he stares first at Sam Labovic and then at Owen Coyle. Cuvallo sees Sam Labovic

pick up the twenty-inch black carryall by his feet and follow the manager back across the lobby and through the
same door down the far wall to his left. Owen Coyle stays
where he is, eyes glued to the desk clerk. Armand Cuvallo
stays where he is, eyes glued to Owen Coyle and feeling
like he's going to be sick.

Not again, not now.

He takes a deep breath—*breathe, you bastard.* Jesus. Sam
Labovic doesn't want any fucking around. And here he is, or
a part of him anyway, that's starting to. Got to keep it
together. He would much fucking prefer to be back in the
housekeeping room again, that's for sure, away from all
these people and the Muzak wafting down from those fucking little speakers hidden somewhere in the ceiling, playing
"Bridge Over Troubled-Fucking-Water"—lord almighty. And
that lady sitting in the padded mauve lounge chair two
down, snorting and wheezing into a hanky, sighing *tsk-tsk*
over and over about something—and the people walking
back and forth and glancing over—suspicious nosey bastards
who just can't leave a guy alone to stand around in a hotel
fucking lobby minding his own fucking business.

He shuts his eyes; this he can do for a moment and not feel
he's attracting attention. His feet seem weighted to the floor.
He sways; it's not dark at all with his eyes shut but a bright
mixture of reds and yellows, like coloured inks dropped on
water, snaking and oscillating on the shiny surface. His eyes
open just in time to watch a chubby guy in a scuffed western

outfit and battered cowboy hat come hobbling through the main doors, making toward the elevators. Bandages peek out from under the cowboy hat and the poor bastard seems to have trouble walking. He passes in front of Armand Cuvallo, his left leg jack-knifing into his abdomen in an obviously uncontrolled movement as his face twists with pain, and Armand Cuvallo forgets for the moment his own rising panic, feeling some amenity for a fellow disability sufferer, although this poor bastard's is physical rather than psychological. And Armand Cuvallo watches after the struggling body, welling sympathy, and absently reads the inscription in red scrawled across the back of the hat. Jesus. *What a fucking thing to do to a spastic.*

* * *

Harry Pazik, on the other hand, is almost getting used to his own more recent physical abnormalities. Since leaving the hospital he's felt like a man in control, a man who of all men knows exactly what he's doing, albeit with a few complications listed earlier back at the hospital by the good doctor, and now with a few parts of the original master plan (he senses there *was* originally a master plan of some kind) admittedly missing. He has his room card at the ready even before the elevator doors slide open; he's way ahead of himself. He's even managed for the most part to detach from his body, abandoning it to its pain and torment. There is only one thing of importance at the moment, only one thing.

He dances and jerks his way down the hallway, leaning up against the doorjamb of Room 414. He fumbles with the card; it slides in without too much of a struggle. He glances at his watch—two-twenty-five—the game is still only in the first quarter. Good thing that cabby finally got it on the radio. Just before they pulled up to the hotel, some guy called Shank, or Shunk or something, for Toronto, fumbled the ball on Toronto's eleven-yard line and Mad Joe Mezzaroba had picked it up and lumbered it in for a touchdown. If things kept up like that, by god, the Stamps were going to do it. The Stamps were gonna be champs.

The door to Room 414 swings to, and Harry lurches in and releases a cry as his leg jack-knifes in its now familiar but mind-numbing pattern. He nearly trips on an empty coffee cup and reams of newspapers left on the floor—jesus christ, aren't the maids supposed to clean these things up? And who made the mess, anyway, he sure as heck didn't. This'd be a great time to break an ankle. No time to call room service and give them an earful, but they'll hear about it after the game. Damn sure they'll hear about it. He is not an animal, a beast of some kind content to wallow in its own filth. No sir, buddy.

A beeline now for the six-drawer cherry laminate dresser. Underwear and socks, shirts, and other clothing get launched across the room. The entire top drawer is pulled out and tipped onto the bed. He can hear the breathing—wild, forced—of someone short of breath. And cursing through clenched teeth.

Another drawer is pulled and dumped, more clawing through articles of clothing.

Here . . . no, there . . . no . . . HERE*!*

And he stands triumphant in the panel mirror, holding the ticket high as the fire alarm in the hall goes off for the sixteenth time that week.

* * *

Around the corner, just six or so blocks away as the crow flies, Jorgen Thrapp welcomes, for the moment, the darkness and relative insulation of the Queen Elizabeth Theatre. He knows that the cards have been dealt; it's all out of his hands. The game will soon be over and fortunes will rise or fall with the outcome. His own odds favour Toronto, but not by much. He'd ditched the last of his betting sheets by eight-thirty the night before, before getting drunk, and now all he has to do is make it through the last-minute walk-through of *La Traviata.* Some Valium and Fiorinal helped and he is once again able to converse in complete sentences. Ron Kanavrous sits in the row in front of him, ironing out minor details of the lighting, munching hard on a four-cheese calzone, while on stage Sophia Fugeta (as the courtesan Violetta) and Heiner Blume (as her boyfriend Alfredo), more or less mumble and sleepwalk their way through their parts without costume. Kristy Kibsey is managing cues, due to the absence of the Fat Man, who at last report was tucked snugly in his own bed, heavily sedated and with a broken right arm. Much heated debate ensued following the death of the tuba player but it was decided that "the show must go on," Sophia Fugeta being the most adamant about not allowing anything to mess with her scheduling for the season. The Fat Man himself had sent a fax to the cast and crew stating his remorse over the unfortunate turn of events but added that he could see no plausible reason for cancelling the event—it was, after all, *Opening Night of the Opera Season.* He'd signed it, "Your Chum."

Ron Kanavrous babbles into his headset, bits of calzone settling in his lap. The lights change in compliance with his instructions. Beside him Jorgen Thrapp drifts in and out of a private fog, still experiencing periodic rushes of anxiety and drug withdrawal. Onstage, Violetta invites the young Alfredo to sing at her party. Alfredo accepts. "*Brindisi. Libiamo, libiamo,*" mumbles Heiner Blume, fingers playing with his cravat.

Jorgen Thrapp sneers inwardly, remembering the seedless oranges. Ron Kanavrous has turned around and is waving two fifty-dollar bills in his face. "Are you there? Are you there, Mr. Thrapp. What the hell's the matter with you?"

"Sorry."

"You look pale, ill."

"I'm fine."

"Want to go lie down or something?"

"Hey, no . . . what's up?"

"Scotch. And get out a piece of paper. Some seafood *Fra Diavolo* this time. I'm starving."

"*Frad*-what?"

"*Fra D-ia-volo*. Shrimp, mussels and calamari. And make sure it's in the red wine sauce, not the white."

"Red, not white." He feels his stomach turn as onstage, Violetta has fainted, and Alfredo reaches out a hand to catch her. "*Un di felice eterea*," drones Heiner Blume.

Ron Kanavrous is waving another fifty. "Make it two bottles. Forties."

Jorgen takes the third bill and walks gratefully up the aisle towards the doors. It might be good to get out of the theatre; the atmosphere has been getting a little repressive. He'll go the long way, hit the liquor store on Alberni in the West End and catch the deli on the way back. Take his time. At the door to the lobby he can hear the poor messed-up Alfredo confessing to Violetta his undying love.

"*Ah, fors e'lui*," replies Sophia Fugeta.

15

Encouraged Optimism

A RMAND CUVALLO IS STILL WATCHING the door that
Sam Labovic and the man he assumes is the hotel
manager have just gone into when the fire alarm goes off.
He leaps, straight up, unhooking the Browning pump from
its strap underneath his own multi-striped and gaudy-
coloured outdoorsy looking jacket. At the stadium, Bogdan
Michaldo, or something, completes an up-the-centre pass
to Dexter Partman for a Toronto twenty-six-yard touchdown and the crowd goes crazy. Up Georgia Street in the
Queen Elizabeth Theatre, Ron Kanavrous is dying for a
drink of scotch, unhappy with the profusion of blue tint
streaming down from the floodlights on stage left, as
Violetta renounces her old way of life and announces plans
to move in with Alfredo, much to the displeasure of

Alfredo's father, played by baritone Willard Stuttz, who, as many in the know have noticed, has a name much like a football player's.

At the main desk of the Hyatt Regency, Owen Coyle swings around at the sound of the fire alarm, a thick finger tightening around the trigger of the Mossberg through a hole cut in his coat pocket. He glances quickly over at Armand Cuvallo, then to the same door Sam Labovic and the hotel manager have gone into. Mike Hatskill, not really surprised by the sound of the fire alarm after the past week, suddenly finds himself unobserved. His hands that have been engaged in a nervous wrestling match with each other on the desk now break their grips, one remaining on top to tap its fingers click-click on the spacer key of the computer keyboard and while the other weasels its way down behind the desk to press the small white button hidden there.

Owen Coyle turns back. "Hey asshole. Keep your hands where I can see them. What is that? Fire?"

"Ah, I believe . . ."

"For fucking real?"

"Highly . . . ah . . . doubtful. Been going off like that all week."

"No shit."

"No sir."

"Well, turn the fucker off!"

"Yes, sir. I mean no, sir."

"What?" The barrel of the Mossberg thumps the desk as Owen Coyle leans forward. Mike Hatskill is certain he hears another thump or two from behind his own ribcage as he backs away.

"Can't, sir. Maintenance will turn it off in a minute."

Owen Coyle takes another quick look around the lobby. People are still wandering through as though unaware of anything amiss, and, as people everywhere seem likely to do in the event of a fire alarm, are totally ignoring it. A young couple with their arms looped around each other's waists giggle into each other's faces as they toss their room card on the counter in front of him and wander toward the street. An older couple, the man hesitating a moment and opening a street map between outstretched arms, stop near the desk, the woman's finger moving impatiently over the folds as she explains to him the way they should've gone. Owen Coyle notices a fine layer of sweat beginning to form just below the desk clerk's hairline. And he's begun to sweat too; and over against the far wall, although Owen Coyle can't see it, Armand Cuvallo sweats, and has been doing so for some time. Still on his feet, he is experiencing a sudden wave of dizziness and praying—*jesus*—*not now*— *don't lose it now*—*someone turn that fucker off!*

Cuvallo's eyes travel once again to the door of the administrative offices, looking for a sign of Sam Labovic. They lock in an x-ray stare on the chrome door handle there. The handle is shiny, looks cold, gleams, reflecting light like a small icy meteorite might, mightn't? And the door handle is not moving, not swinging to as it should if the fucking door was being opened. Just still. Closed. Nothing happening. *And whatareya doing in there Labovic? Giving the guy a blowjob?* Then he glimpses one of the two uniformed and armed security guys by the escalators approaching the main desk. He grips the Browning tighter—oh, fuck—Owen's standing there looking so cool. Has he noticed? And, jesus, what's that asshole desk clerk going to pull?

The alarm stops ringing as abruptly as it started and the young gigglers disappear through the door into the street. The old couple near the desk fold their map and with a weary look the man follows his wife to the elevators. The uniformed and armed security guy, when the alarm stops, shrugs and turns, wandering back to his buddy. And Armand Cuvallo moves over to the corner to stand next to a huge big-leafed plant just as the spastic in the western suit comes out of the elevator and Cuvallo watches once more the poor guy's agonized dance across the lobby. The sight of him again is just as distressing; in fact, everyone is beginning to look a little fucked-over. He raises his gaze to the ceiling, a safer and less threatening place. There's a quaint Victorian motif of vines or something carved up there in a vast and subtle relief, and it snakes its way over to and along the deep crown moldings, quite detailed, might even be clusters of grapes in the design. Now, who would even notice that, he thinks, yanking his finger off the trigger of the Browning under his coat before he blows his fucking foot off.

*   *   *

Outside, down the street and around the corner, Jorgen Thrapp walks briskly along Dunsmuir. He whistles, attempting what even he regards as a pretty lame attempt at nonchalance. He'd thought to take his time but has been unable to reign in his jangled nerves, which have manifested themselves into a near-gallop since he left the theatre. Walking slow—"sauntering"—seems counter to his present mental and physical state. But the day is crisp and clear. The sky, unmarred by pollution, is a deep baby-blanket blue. And it's here, under a clear cuddly sky along Dunsmuir Street in Vancouver's downtown, that Jorgen Thrapp is at last able (in his own mind, at least) to absolve himself of responsibility for anything uncomfortable that has happened over the last few days. The good weather itself encourages optimism and he's able to attribute any recent horrors to the accumulative pressures of opening night of the opera season and the general craziness of Grey Cup week. These events have nothing directly to do with him, Jorgen Thrapp the person, and they will pass (this he concludes rightly), and he'll be none the worse for wear (and this, of course, he doesn't).

He swings his arms, something he never does. He smiles, remembering his surprise the day before upon finding a note from opera diva Sophia Fugeta. She wished to see him. He had no idea what for. He entertained a few sexual fantasies before knocking on her dressing room door. Anything can happen in theatre, and does. They're all crazier than shithouse rats and why should the star of *La Traviata* be any different? He was a bit disappointed when Ms. Fugeta did not ask him to remove his clothes but instead asked in a thick accent for some downers— Percocet, Dionin—whatever. He cringes even now, unable to explain why at that moment he leaned forward with a sweeping bow and answered gravely, "Of course, Madame. Consider it done." What an idiot. But that's what theatre can do to you. Everybody starts acting, even the stage crew can become dramatic, saying things like "Tote that street prop over here would you," rather than "Put the fucker there for now." But all is made worthwhile when Kristy Kibsey delivers a request from Heiner Blume for some of the same. "A few Percocet needed, Miss Kibsey, for the nerves," he'd said. And Kristy, of course, had attempted to oblige, tracking Jorgen down and asking him to make the delivery this morning, which he had done, saddled with two envelopes labelled respectively "Madame Fugeta" and "Monsieur Blume," the envelope for Madame containing the calming Percocet and some Dionin, the envelope for Monsieur containing the speeder Benzedrine.

See you on the moon, Mr. Blume.

He walks on in rising spirits, crossing at the light and heading up Burrard towards the West End. A siren breaks the spell, coming up from behind. The squeal of tires as a police car roars past. Another patrol car follows as a tired tan Chevy Sprint makes its way slowly by in the opposite direction. A block and a half ahead, near the Hyatt Regency, more sirens and screeching of tires can be heard. A loud crash. Almost immediately, there's a series of short-clipped pops, like firecrackers, and something makes light tapping noises on the road to his left.

He stops walking.

A man on the sidewalk across the street stops too, standing just as stupidly, looking over, a round black hole where his mouth hangs open. Jorgen Thrapp, hating above all to look the ass, decides he doesn't care what anybody thinks and lies flat on his belly on the sidewalk. He sees the man across the street follow his example, to hell with his cool too. It's dawned on him what those tapping noises are, although he's never even been *close* to a bullet, not even a stationary one. It is strange nonetheless. Nothing like the long, drawn-out, guitar-like twangs that ricochets have in the movies. There's the effects of theatre again. Art only imitates life, and badly at that.

The firecracker pops and the tapping noises stop, but the sirens keep coming. He remains prone on the sidewalk, no longer convinced that all things will pass. It's a mean, hideous, dangerous world and only an asshole would walk along thinking everything was okay. Maybe the Owl-man is simply an omen of some kind, an omen of, say, an early and violent death, like being shot while tripping your way to buy a couple of forties of scotch and a deli dish you can't pronounce, let alone spell, for the lighting designer of *La Traviata*. He can learn from this, he decides while gripping the concrete with elbows, toes, kneecaps, and chin, about to pick up some nauseous assortment of shrimp, mussels, and calamari in red (not the white) wine sauce. Yes, he can learn again what he's known since day one, and never forget it: there is dick-all percentage in looking for the good, the reliable, the sure thing. It's more in keeping with the world and its ways to maintain a suspicious eye peeled for the inevitable—the bad, the ugly, the sneaking-up-from-behind-to-bite-you-on-the-ass—the Big Mean Surprise.

16

Ivan Jornofsky

W HEN HARRY PAZIK, once more in stride (of sorts), at last makes his way out through the main doors of the hotel, the taxi is gone.

"I told that bastard to wait!"

A tour group, standing huddled along the curb, eyes him nervously. Harry Pazik, oblivious to the stares, grimaces again as his left leg jack-knifes once again into his abdomen. A tan Chevy Sprint hatchback with a Rent-A-Ride sticker on its windshield pulls into the passenger area and Dezura Shapiro gets out from the driver's side, wearing a brightly coloured African-style robe and huge purple-framed sunglasses.

"Dezura—*Dezura!* The game. I'm late for the game!"

"Harry, my god. What are you doing here?"

"Dezura. You *must* help me."

"Harry, I think you should still be in the hospital."

"I'm okay, Dezura . . . I'm fine."

"Frankly, Harry, you look like crap."

"Thank you, Dezura. Thank you very much. I need a ride. A ride to the stadium. Don't think I can make it walking. Look here." He waves his ticket in her face. The doorman comes over.

"Ma'am. You can't park here."

"Park? Who's parked? I'll just be a minute."

The doorman nods politely; he too has watched that chest cross the lobby on several occasions.

Harry intones, "Dezura—for christ's sake . . ."

"I'm sorry, Harry. But I'm in a hurry too. There's a wine and cheese opening at Slat's Gallery and the artist, whoever he is, is going to be there. I've got to grab some things and run along. You should really be in bed or something. I've got to be going. Catch you later."

And Dezura Shapiro in her African-style robe sails into the lobby, leaving in her wake the heavy scent of incense, perfume, and marijuana. Harry Pazik attempts to catch her arm, grimacing once again and grabbing his side as his left leg jackknifes, taking a few faltering steps toward the tour group, who in turn shuffle back out of range. The doorman moves back toward the doors, peering after Dezura Shapiro, appearing intent and solicitous, and frankly, not wishing to deal with the tubby guy carrying on outside.

Harry Pazik now circles the Chevy Sprint; the keys are still in it, the motor running. Opening the door on the driver's side, he winces as he crawls into the seat. The doorman strides over and Harry smiles horribly up at him from the window.

"It's okay, my man. The lady wishes me to move it. In case that tour group's bus comes along."

"Are you sure—"

"It's okay. I take full responsibility. I'm staying at the hotel. Ivan Jornofsky. Room 311."

The doorman hesitates. But something about the bandaged head, the watery frantic eyes and battered cowboy hat with the lipstick inscription scrawled across the back . . . it's not his job to referee a bunch of crazy bastards over the outcome of a football game. He walks away, hearing a yelp as Harry reaches for the gear shift, just as nine blocks away in BC Place Stadium, another yelp is heard as Bobby Mashtaler successfully sticks a finger in the right eye of Toronto wide receiver Dexter Herman on the Calgary goal line, sending him to the dressing room for what will later be reported as only rudimentary medical attention.

Harry Pazik feels a hundred needles dance in his chest as he slowly engages the clutch; what the hell is Dezura Shapiro doing with a manual shift? At this moment, a burly guy in a gaudy coloured jacket comes running out of the hotel doors in a low crouch holding a tote bag close to his left side, a big Commander Colt gripped tightly in his right

140 • TOM OSBORNE

hand. Sirens sound from the near-distance as the guy with
the gun passes the tour group. Fourteen voices shriek as
one, as fourteen sets of eyes spy the Colt .45. The group
retreats in panic from this new threat, and seeks the open
street. Sam Labovic catches a chaotic glimpse of flailing
arms and legs, bodies falling over each other and blue-
veined thighs thrashing the air from under raised print
skirts. Inside the tan Chevy Sprint hatchback, Harry Pazik
plays madly with the buttons on the radio. Blasts of static,
various spits of music. The passenger door flies open, and
Sam Labovic is there, jumping in, and putting the muzzle of
the Colt Commander up against Harry's heavily veined
temple. An announcer's voice comes in raspy over the roar
of a crowd through the single speaker.

"Got it!" shouts Harry Pazik, turning to look at Sam
Labovic and taking the muzzle of the Colt in the eye.
"Ow."

"You think *that* hurt?" shouts Sam Labovic. *"Drive,
buddy!"*

"Wha—"

"Drive, *asshole!"*

Harry Pazik blinks down the muzzle of the .45, the
sirens louder now, coming fast up Burrard. Harry grinds the
gears as Sam Labovic slams the door, and gives him a stiff
rap on the head with the barrel of the Commander Colt.
"Go!"

"Go!" echoes Harry, his foot tromping the gas pedal.

The Sprint leaps forward as out of the corner of his eye Harry sees the side glass door to the lobby disappear. At the same time he hears a brain-shattering boom and the barrel of the Commander Colt once more connects with his head.

"Stop!" shouts Sam Labovic.

"Stop!" Harry Pazik shouts back.

His ribs jar up against the steering wheel, his left leg spasms into the dashboard. Sam Labovic reaches around and throws open the back door as Owen Coyle sprints out through the opening where the glass door to the lobby used to be, waving the Mossberg. He discharges another blast from the Mossberg into the air, causing the tour group to tumble screaming to the sidewalk. Owen Coyle dives into the back seat of the Chevy.

"GO!" shouts Owen Coyle.

Sam Labovic pounds the head of Harry Pazik. "GO!"

Harry Pazik fights the gears, yells, "YES! GO!" and trounces down on the gas pedal as the Chevy Sprint shoots forward in a careening horseshoe turn out of the drop-off area and onto Burrard Street, swerving across two lanes and heading down toward the harbour.

"Not too fast!" shouts Sam Labovic, ducking down. "Pass 'em easy."

Two patrol cars roar by in the opposite direction, coming up from the harbour and turning into the Hyatt. Harry drives the rental car slowly down Burrard to Hastings Street, obeying orders from Sam Labovic. On the radio he hears that Bogdan Michaldo, or something, has handed off to Marble Caser on a fifteen-yard end-around for another Toronto touchdown. He groans. Sam Labovic keeps the Commander Colt trained on him as Owen Coyle lies puffing across the back seat, reloading the Mossberg and trying to figure out what went wrong. He pumps a shell into the chamber and quietly reads the inscription on the back of the driver's hat.

17

Feelings of Surprise and Relief

As Jorgen Thrapp gets to his feet from where he's lain chin to pavement on Burrard Street at the sound of gunshots and the tick-tick of slugs nailing the asphalt beside him, nine blocks away in BC Place Stadium, Mad Joe Mezzaroba is hunched over at the Calgary Stampeder's bench, throwing up into a bucket placed there by the bench boy, who's standing off to one side trying to concentrate on the action on the field so as not to be sick himself. Mad Joe received a hit in the stomach that agitated a severe hangover, a by-product of the illicit and clandestine debauch with Bobby Mashtaler the night before. Across the field,

high above the fifty-yard line in the VIP box, Mayor Dusty
Moons, with binoculars focused on Mad Joe, grins his shiny
whites.

Jorgen Thrapp does not feel too well either, as he makes
his way slowly past the Hyatt. One of the two police cars
that passed him moments ago is straddled across the pas-
senger-loading zone in front of the main doors. The other is
up on the curb, the front end wrapped around a light pole
and the windshield blown out. Two more police cars block
the exit onto Burrard and the body of a man, a brightly
coloured jacket twisted up over his head, lays bloodied and
unmoving midway between. Some guests and hotel staff are
seated or lying spread-eagled on the sidewalk where they
likely dove for cover. Others are slowly getting to their feet,
but nobody's saying much. A woman's muffled screams can
be heard from inside the lobby as more sirens approach.
He's being told to move on by a police officer directing foot
traffic along the sidewalk, "Nothing to gawk at here, fella,"
and Jorgen Thrapp keeps moving, but gawking too—bullet-
riddled cop cars and a bullet-riddled body, who wouldn't?—
and reaches into his pant pocket to pull out a scrap of paper.
And reads aloud: "Seafood *Fra Diavolo*."

A look back at the body is a reminder: "In the *red* wine
sauce, not the white."

*   *   *

Owen Coyle hears the sirens first, and listens, staring just past Mike Hatskill's head at the clock on the wall above. About the same time, Armand Cuvallo hears a static call-code come from the direction of the two uniformed and armed security guys standing by the escalators, then sees one of them speak into his radio and wait for a reply. The other guy leans over and says something, which must have been funny because they both laugh, and Armand Cuvallo stands tighter against the wall, hears the laughter faint but with a resonance (to him, anyway) as if he was standing in a huge, acoustically perfect amphitheatre. At that moment he sees the chrome door handle down the way, the one reflecting light like a small icy meteorite, move—as it finally fucking should—as the fucking door opens at last, swinging inward and out of sight as Sam Labovic steps out.

Sam Labovic had become aware of the sirens growing louder at the same time Owen Coyle did, at the same time Cuvallo picked up the garbled static from the uniformed and armed security guy's radio. Cuvallo sees Sam coming straight for the main doors, the black tote bag gripped tightly in his left hand. The two security guys stop listening to the radio and stop laughing. They look suddenly alert, unholstering their sidearms. One mumbles something to the other and they both start for the main desk and Owen Coyle.

Armand Cuvallo starts forward but is stalled momentarily by a wave of nausea. Owen Coyle remains motionless at the front desk, aware of Sam Labovic walking by with the tote bag in a fast, but not too fast, walk to the main doors. The sirens are very loud now, and there can only be one place they're headed.

Owen Coyle glances over at Cuvallo, sees him wavering, face drawn and pale, and Owen Coyle doesn't like it. Armand Cuvallo sees the uniformed and armed security guys making for the front desk (who Owen Coyle doesn't see) and he doesn't like *that*. The Browning appears from under his jacket and he turns, blowing a hole in the wall behind him. Shit—*don't shoot the walls*—but it's too late now. The sound of the explosion at least stops the two uniformed and armed security guys a few yards from the front desk, as intended, and they dive to the floor for cover. Owen Coyle flips the Mossberg out and blows a hole in the ceiling above the main desk, bits of Victorian motif, vines and maybe grapes, raining down. Back in the administrative offices, all Merrill Swann can think to do is dive under his own desk having had no trouble doing what he'd been told to do by the guy with the big gun. "Do what you're told and no fucking around," the guy'd said. And Merrill Swann, to the best of his knowledge, had not fucked around in the slightest but had co-operated fully, which was painfully apparent by the open and empty hotel safe. Bye-bye to the assorted jewellery and other valuables belonging to guests, the eighty to a hundred thousand hard ridiculous cash belonging to the eccentric Mr. Blume who was residing in one of the luxury suites, not to mention the hotel's own fairly substantial cash float and the opera diva Ms. Fugeta's (also residing in a luxury suite) extensive jewellery collection, including some 2.0 carat high-clarity diamond solitaires in eighteen-carat gold settings that alone run close to twenty thousand each. Still at the main desk, Owen Coyle pumps the Mossberg and levels it at the two uniformed and armed security guys who lie belly-down on the floor, trying to squeeze behind a couple of potted plants. Armand Cuvallo stands unmoving, back against the wall he's blown apart, watching the mad exodus of hotel guests out the lobby doors. The desk clerk is nowhere in sight and he sees Owen Coyle move forward a few steps with a warning to the security guys. Owen Coyle picks up their revolvers, which they slid across the carpet to him as directed, and Coyle tosses them back behind the front desk from where Cuvallo hears a thin cry of pain and now knows where the desk clerk has disappeared to.

Owen Coyle moves fast now, ordering the two uniformed and now unarmed security guys around to the elevators and forcing them in, pushing the button for the top floor. He then makes for the side doors, waving the Mossberg back and forth at waist level, warning people to back off, which they are eager to do. Armand Cuvallo remains by the far wall, struggling to keep himself together and not black out. Some whimpering and screaming can be heard from people cowering behind tables and chairs strewn about the lobby. Sam Labovic draws his Colt as he passes by and breaks into a run at the main lobby doors. Owen Coyle signals to Cuvallo, motioning him to follow, but Cuvallo seems not to notice. Coyle gains the top step down to the side doors and hesitates, looking once more over at Cuvallo. "C'mon! Get the fuck moving!"

Armand Cuvallo jerks, staring anxiously around the lobby. In a sudden panic, he dashes across the carpet away from Coyle and toward the escalators. The sirens outside are coming up the street toward the front entrance area. Owen Coyle shakes his head and turns, squeezing off a round from the Mossberg and sending the glass doors to oblivion. He pumps the Mossberg once and bounds through the now-empty doorframe.

*   *   *

Armand Cuvallo stops at the foot of the escalators. He can smell seafood from the restaurant on the mezzanine above. Some kind of chowder, maybe. It's not pleasant. He gasps for air—jesus christ, but nothing ever seems to get much better. A grey-haired woman catches his attention, looking up bug-eyed from behind a chair on his right and babbling hysterically, offering up her purse. Armand Cuvallo stares at her dumbly, wanting to just blow her head off and stop the racket. Then he's off, back across the lobby toward the main doors and out into the daylight as a police car screeches into the hotel parkway. The Browning comes up and explodes, lord god almighty, and Armand Cuvallo watches the windshield of the car disappear as the two cops inside dive for the floorboards underneath the dash. The car bumps up the curb and comes to a crunching stop at the main doors. Another police car just behind it swerves onto the sidewalk, wrapping its front end around a lamp post. There's no sign of Sam Labovic or Owen Coyle as he pumps the Browning again, turning away from the street to the mouth of the underground parkade. He sees the ramp heading down and two uniformed security guards coming up. He turns back to the street, and feels surprise upon realizing his anxiety has strangely disappeared. It's all the standing around that does it, all the waiting before having to shoot holes in walls or make mad dashes across hotel lobbies. Gives time for one's phobias, no matter how minor, to grow, nourish themselves, and eat one fucking alive. That's when the panic comes. But now that something is finally happening, he feels almost happy. Two more police cars have blocked the drive. He raises the Browning. Someone yells, a tenth of a second before Armand Cuvallo obliterates his second windshield of the afternoon. Other shots follow as Armand Cuvallo, who is 37 years old, 6 feet, 2 and 1/2 inches tall, and weighs 165 pounds, 7 ounces, pumps once more and spins, marvelling at a wash of calmness he's never felt when alive, and collapses on the asphalt with four holes in his chest.

*   *   *

Along Georgia Street at the Queen Elizabeth Theatre in the walk-through of *La Traviata*, the tragedy of Armand Cuvallo is mirrored by another tragedy of loss, though less violent, as Alfredo finds Violetta's farewell letter. But unlike Armand Cuvallo, who is beyond consolation, Alfredo is comforted by his father, who talks of their home in Provence.

"*Di provenza il mar,*" actually sings Willard Stuttz (even though it is only a rehearsal).

2:00 Carat Size High Clarity
Diamond in Gold Setting

18

"Hank"

AFTER LISTENING TO the end-around play to Toronto halfback Marble Caser, Harry Pazik nearly drives off the road. Sam Labovic reaches over and turns off the radio, while at the same time debating the usefulness of giving the goomba in the cowboy hat another rap on the head with the .45.

"Watch what you're doin', Tex!"

It's been less than a minute since Sam Labovic came running out of the Hyatt Regency lobby and grabbed the first car he'd seen, but it's been time enough to see that this bird behind the wheel is either missing a few screws or is simply too stunned with fear. As for Harry Pazik, goomba and bird, he's in deep shock, flitting in and out of a pain-driven reality (*twisting of the brain structures and blood vessels ... break-*

down of the normal flow of messages within the brain . . .).
Part of him is still back at the hotel, knowing there's somewhere he's supposed to be, somewhere he's vaguely aware is
within walking distance for anyone not physically impaired.
The other part of him is now driving to another somewhere
in Dezura Shapiro's rented, manual shift, one-radio-speaker-
only rental car. And this latter part does what he's told if he's
smart and takes orders from the guy with the big gun. That's
his job.

Sam Labovic sits grim in the front seat. It's impossible to
tell from what directions all the sirens are coming; the
whole downtown area seems crawling with them. As soon
as one fades another comes on, getting louder as it flies by
on an adjacent street. He fires directions to the goomba;
Harry Pazik obeys, doing his best at his new job and turning when told to, changing lanes and slowing down and
speeding up but always maintaining a cautionary speed.
And it seems that just when he's getting the hang of it, the
guy with the big gun orders him to pull into a public parking lot and park. And keep his mouth shut.

Sam Labovic turns to the back seat. "You okay?"

Owen Coyle sits up. "Yeah. I'm okay."

"Look, we'll use the key Marty gave me. I don't like it
but we've still got to dump this stuff and stick to the plan.
No other choice, the place is crawling. I don't know how
Armand made out. Didn't see him. He doesn't know
enough to cause trouble anyway. I don't think."

"He didn't look so good last I saw. Was bolting for the escalators for christ's sake."

"That's not so good."

"No. Not so good."

"Well, we got to chance it."

Labovic turns back to Harry. "Okay, you. What's your name?"

Harry Pazik hears a name swim up through the confused mist of his concussion . . .

"Hank."

"Hank, what?"

"Hank . . ."

"Okay. Hank'll do. Everything's going to be fine, Hank. Understand? Don't give me any attitude or fucking around and everything'll be fine."

Harry nods, looking blankly at the ticket he's pulled out of his pocket. "I got this ticket here . . ."

"Shut the fuck up, Hank."

Harry shuts up, once more numb with pain and vaguely wondering how far they are from the stadium and not knowing why he cares.

"Get out, Hank."

Harry climbs out the driver's side, leaning on the door as his left leg jack-knifes in the air. The guy with the big gun looks at him strangely. "You okay?"

"I'm fine," he wheezes, looking back just as strangely. "I've had a slight accident . . . somewhere . . ."

"You're telling us," says Sam Labovic, and guides him by the arm. Owen Coyle carries the black tote bag as they thread their way through the cars in the parking lot.

Harry stumbles painfully along, feeling more an observer than a participant. The mental effort to put it all together is too great. His head throbs under the bandages, christ, one of them, Hank or Harry, did take quite a whack. And what was it that had come bouncing out of the sky? And he had better make a call to Celia; Celia's somehow important. A vague recollection of a cell phone left somewhere, tossed carelessly, maybe Celia's on the speed dial. She could be the key to it all. And there's something big happening today, and Harry or Hank should be there. The Grey Cup, yes, that's it. Big game. Short-term memories seem to be almost in order. Something that doctor said back at the hospital—um, nope—can't remember. The Grey Cup, the Stamps are gonna be champs. That's important. And he, Hank, is missing it. And what about the guy with the big gun, he and the shorter guy have got something important to do too and Hank—or Harry—is supposed to help. And the guy with the big gun doesn't want any attitude or fucking around; that will be worth remembering if nothing else is.

They leave the parking lot, cross the street, and approach the back doors of a building unfamiliar to Harry. A loading bay. A moving truck is backed in. And a set of bright orange doors. The man with the big gun moves up the steps to the orange doors, and Harry follows. The shorter guy brings up the rear behind them and looks back across the parking lot. Sam Labovic inserts a key and yanks the door open, pushes Harry ahead, and Harry's eyes read a sign above the doorway:

ORCHESTRA & STAGE CREW ONLY
ALL OTHERS USE MAIN DOORS

* * *

Jorgen Thrapp returns to the theatre and heads directly for Ron Kanavrous's office. He's carrying two bags, one from the liquor store and one from the deli. He can hear shouts and hollering down the hall where the maintenance and stage crews are watching the Grey Cup on TV in the common room. He pauses to look in and ask the score. A pudgy guy in a rumpled western jacket and wearing a battered white Stetson turns to say, "Fourteen–seven, Toronto." Two burly guys sitting on either side of him turn and smile, as Jorgen Thrapp smiles dumbly back and reads the inscription on the back of the cowboy guy's hat. He continues down the hall, entering Ron's office and plunking the bags down on the desk. Ron Kanavrous looks up and pulls a forty-ounce bottle of scotch from one of the bags. From the other, Jorgen Thrapp unloads two corned-beef sandwiches and one of ham, a meat pie, three sausage rolls, four croissants (two with cheese, two with onions), a Greek salad, a pound of coleslaw, one large soup of the day (minestrone), some pickled herring, a slab of tongue, and a three-foot salami ring.

"What the fuck is all this?" says Ron Kanavrous.

"You won't freaking guess what happened on the way to the deli," says Jorgen Thrapp.

*   *   *

Sam Labovic and Owen Coyle are thinking much along the same lines, sitting on either side of Harry Pazik and watching Grey Cup third-quarter action on TV in the downstairs staff common room of the Queen Elizabeth Theatre. It's a tense moment when they first pass by the door of the common room after entering the theatre. Hank seems to return to himself just as the Calgary quarterback, Sonny Joachim or something, botches a handoff to the fullback Luis Jesus and Toronto recovers the fumble. The room erupts in a roar and Hank is inside and seated before they know it, sitting with the maintenance and stage crews and cheering or jeering the Calgary Stampeders. Sam Labovic and Owen Coyle join him, not sure what else to do, while one floor up, still rehearsing *La Traviata* on stage and in keeping with life imitating art, Alfredo is equally confused as to what to do when Violetta walks into the party on the arm of Baron

Douphol, and Alfredo immediately begins guzzling wine and glaring at her across the room.

One floor down, Harry Pazik begins to guzzle too, accepting a beer offered from one of the maintenance crew while glaring at the events taking place on the TV screen. Sam Labovic and Owen Coyle decline, more concerned with keeping their heads clear and an eye on their hostage. Hank seems to be enjoying himself at least and they look far less conspicuous sitting here than wandering the theatre. And whatever's wrong with this guy, Hank, they decide, it doesn't appear he's going to make any trouble and for now that's all they want. They even allow him to make a few good-natured side bets with the crew just as upstairs in rehearsal, Alfredo, upset with Violetta and the Baron Dauphol, also begins to gamble heavily.

About ten minutes later, a skinny guy with his arms full of what appear to be groceries sticks his head in the doorway, asking the score. Sam Labovic and Owen Coyle tense at the voice, then relax as Hank cordially answers the guy and the guy disappears. Sam Labovic waits ten minutes, gets up and says something into the ear of Owen Coyle. Owen Coyle nods and Sam picks up the tote bag and walks out the door and up the hall. Without much trouble he finds the boiler room, pausing a moment to scan the hallway. Then he pushes the door open, letting it close as another roar erupts faintly from the common room.

Inside the boiler room, he stops again by a smaller door

labelled MAINTENANCE. He passes through to a row of lockers huddled against the far wall and finds the one he wants. Using the numbers Martin gave to him over the phone three days ago, he unlatches the combination lock. The locker door bangs open just as the door to the maintenance room creaks open behind him. He whirls around, dropping the tote bag, his right hand coming up out of his pocket with the added weight of the Commander Colt .45. The skinny guy with the groceries who stuck his head in the door of the common room earlier stands mesmerized in the doorway of the maintenance room, eyes bugged and glued on the muzzle of the .45. His hands move awkwardly, trying to push something down into his pants and Sam Labovic watches as pills of various colours tumble to the floor, bouncing off the guy's size-twelve Adidas.

19

Acts of Terrorism

WHEN ARMAND CUVALLO blows a hole in the wall, Mike Hatskill does what everyone else in the lobby does. He freezes. When Owen Coyle blows a hole in the ceiling right above him, it's time to move—a flat-out dive to the floor behind the desk with his eyes closed, and wets himself on the way. He hears the cries of terror and confusion that fill the lobby, the pounding of a lot of feet running. He hears a crash, a table lamp probably. Moments later two pistols, silver, come over the desk, one missing his head, one not. He pees again, convinced he's now being beaten by the guy with the shotgun for setting off the alarm. On the third blast, when Owen Coyle sends the side glass doors into outer space, with no fluids left and his fingers dug deep into the carpet, he suddenly finds religion while curled up behind the main desk on the lobby floor of the Hyatt Regency Hotel—*Please, God, get your holier-than-thou shit together and remove all assholes from the premises!* He's even open to trade-offs, silently agreeing to stop gambling, drinking, and ogling the female guests. He will start giving the tips to the bellhops instead of telling the guests he'll see to it and pocketing them himself, and he'll even stop carrying on with that tart who works in the Mosaic Bar & Grille on the second floor (signature restaurant overlooking downtown Vancouver), and, yes, he'll make more time for Mrs. Hatskill and Mike Hatskill Junior.

Moments later, with the shooting over—and consequently any need to keep repenting over too—he pulls himself to his feet and braces himself against the counter, keeping the front of his trousers hidden. At that moment, Armand Cuvallo lunges out the lobby doors, making his run and letting go a blast from the Browning sawed-off. Mike Hatskill makes a sound, somewhere between laughter and a sob, but is afraid to fall back down again; there may be no getting up. Instead he sprawls forward over the countertop, fingers clamped on the outside edge, hanging on.

People who had not fled the lobby at the initial barrage of fire but had instead collapsed or dove to the floor are moving now, free of the initial shock and making with panic-driven speed anywhere that's away from the front doors. Mike Hatskill is now beset by a new, more personal fear, weighing the possibility of making it to Swann's office to get some clean trousers before the cops arrive and start asking questions. Desperation and shame in a mad dash from behind the desk, a three-ring binder of staff schedules pressed protectively over his crotch and that crotch heading for the door of the administrative offices. And he is almost hoping for another gun blast as a diversion as he reaches the door needed, throws it open and enters the inner hallway. Flying on by the smaller offices, there's no one in sight. Then he glimpses the accountant, Barney Kaplan, through a doorway, sitting on the floor of his office, cowering against a filing cabinet, his face hidden behind hands clutching the day's financial statements. Farther along, Liza Botinelli, concierge, sobs in a corner, her always immaculate hairdo now in disarray. A blur is heard whimpering on the right, as Shirley Stamp, Merrill's secretary, curls up under a chair next to the coffee machine, pink mohair sweater bunched over her head exposing white bra, trembling flesh.

He motors past and into Swann's office at the end, closing the door and leaning up against it. The room appears deserted, then from under the desk comes a voice: "Please, don't kill me."

He crouches down and peers at Merrill Swann squatting there. Merrill Swann, tie clenched in teeth, peers back.

"Hatskill."

"Mr. Swann."

"What are you doing here?"

"I need some trousers, sir."

"Trousers?"

"Yes, sir. I've—ah—had an accident."

"Good lord, Hatskill."

"I know, sir."

"The guests . . ."

"Still with their heads down, sir."

"Thank god. Help me out of here. I was looking for my pen, dropped in the confusion."

"Yes, sir."

"How many dead, Hatskill? Wounded? Ready to sue?"

"Can't say, sir. Nobody hurt that I could see."

"Thank christ for that. I heard the sirens. Sounded like a shootout."

"I'm not sure, sir. I was too busy . . . administering to a lady who fainted."

"Like that?"

"No, sir. The . . . ah . . . accident came later. Don't know how it happened, sir. Bloody frightening. Gun went off right in front of me."

"Well, good work, Hatskill. Putting the guests first."

"Thank you, sir."

"There're some trousers in the closet. Should fit. Best I can do. Tidy yourself up and we'll get out there. Not good for the guests to think they've been abandoned."

"Did you find your pen, sir?"

"What?"

"Your pen."

"Oh, yes. Yes, found it. May seem stupid at a time like this, Mr. Hatskill, but one can't go on losing pens. Sloppy. A pen here, a pen there, soon adds up I'll tell you. Overhead goes through the roof. Know how much we spend annually just on paper clips, Mr. Hatskill? No? A helluva lot, I'll tell you. Send your kid to college. Forget the little things and everything falls apart."

"Yes, sir."

"Well, they got it all, Hatskill. Jewellery, money . . . I refused to be a part of it, refused to open the safe . . ."

"Yes, sir."

"Told that thug that I was not the type to be intimidated by acts of terrorism."

"Yes, sir."

"It was only when he threatened to go out there and shoot *you* that I gave in."

"Thank you, sir."

"Yes, no choice, Mr. Hatskill. All set? Now let's get out there."

Merrill Swann and Mike Hatskill head back through the outer offices, Swann reassuring the office staff still cowering in their hiding places along the way. On seeing the manager emerge from the administrative offices into the lobby, people rush forward with a deluge of questions. Mike Hatskill avoids the crowd and walks purposefully to the main desk, his socks more than visible in the sizeable gap between the cuffs of Merrill Swann's borrowed pants and the tops of his shoes. Some people are still picking themselves up off the floor and crawling out of hiding places. Merrill Swann heads for the main doors followed by the crowd as Mike Hatskill sees the ample bosom of Dezura Shapiro bounce around the corner from the elevators. He watches them bounce across the lobby to the crowd now gathered at the main doors where once outside, they bounce up to the doorman, who shakes his head. They then turn to a police officer, where they stop and proceed to bounce out the make of the rental car that has just been stolen.

20

Crazier Than the Rest of Us

Six or so blocks away in the Queen Elizabeth Theatre, events unfolding in the operatic world of *La Traviata* are almost as ugly as they are in the real world of the Hyatt Regency. Alfredo finally loses his temper and, in a fit of jealousy, flings his gambling money in the face of Violetta while hurling insults at her in front of the other guests. Directly below, one floor down in the real world of the theatre common room, Harry Pazik is holding his head in his hands and hurling insults at the entire Calgary Stampeders football team. The maintenance crew are on their feet, cursing that bastard Bogdan Michaldo, or something, who's just hit Dexter Hartman for a forty-five-yard completed pass and another Toronto touchdown. Harry Pazik feels sick, if not confused. He is not with both feet planted firmly on the ground here. Deviating thoughts flit across, over, and through his mind on jolts of pain, as he is once again aware there are seats somewhere else, somewhere else where he should be sitting—and who's Hank?— or Bogdan Michaldo for that matter? He feels for a moment within the grasp of something . . . a picture, familiar . . . a ranch-style home . . . a river . . . a distant mountain range, pale purple . . . and a bowling league. The terms "amortization period" and "bare land strata" make themselves heard. He turns to Owen Coyle.

"You know . . . I've always been serious about my fiduciary responsibility . . . when arranging property . . . and housing transactions . . ." And he reaches down for another beer, his leg jack-knifing.

Owen Coyle sits stoically beside him, gives him a glance. He is unnerved to see what appear to be tears in Hank's eyes after this last statement. But no one seems overly concerned with their presence as yet and that's a christly relief. And Hank still doesn't seem totally cognizant of his situation, which is another relief. Maybe this is as good as it gets for this guy, maybe it's all the poor yahoo can handle. And thinking this, Owen Coyle has to admit, he himself isn't much better off. What, for instance, does he know about his own situation at this point? "Say what, Hank?" he says.

"Gross debt service ratio," says Harry Pazik, his attention again focussed on the TV.

Owen Coyle looks away, decides to let these comments pass. Who knows? And should one ask? Probably not.

Sam Labovic appears in the doorway, still carrying the tote bag. Owen Coyle doesn't like his expression as Labovic sits down and leans across Hank, grabbing a beer for himself. If Sam Labovic's having a beer at a time like this, something's wrong. Somebody or something was fucking around.

A chair scrapes along the floor; Sam Labovic takes a couple of long swallows from the can of beer and is on his feet again, moving behind Coyle's chair and leaning down to Coyle's ear. Harry's aware of whispering and the guy with the big gun putting the tote bag down at the quiet guy's feet. Then the guy with the big gun vanishes out the door again, leaving the quiet guy with a half-finished beer and the tote bag.

Once outside the common room Sam Labovic heads down the hall in the opposite direction from the boiler room. He takes a flight of stairs two at a time and proceeds quickly down another hallway, looking for the right door. He finds it, gives three knocks, then another, and Jorgen Thrapp opens it.

*   *   *

Back in the real world of the common room, life for Owen Coyle is getting screwier. This Hank guy is now guzzling beers one after another and there's no telling where that might lead. The tote bag is wedged between his feet and he's on his second beer himself. It doesn't seem like a smart thing to do but he has to do something, christ, this is not the way it'd been planned. Then again, nothing ever happens as planned. They were just supposed to drop the shit off, put it in a locker somewhere, and Martin the musician would take it out after the performance that evening when the heat was off. Simple goddamned enough but now it was turning into some kind of epic adventure, complete with shoot-outs and wacky sidekicks, but a noticeable lack of heroes.

It's five minutes and twenty-five seconds later that Sam Labovic comes back into the room. And Owen Coyle knows it's five minutes and twenty-five seconds because he's timed him, timed him like mad. Sam Labovic is dressed in black formal evening wear.

"Okay, Sam," Owen Coyle leans over. "What gives— what the fuck are you doing?"

"Just do as I say for now."

"What's with the get-up? Don't get me wrong, you look great. But wouldn't you rather be shitting your pants in something less extravagant, cuz that's what I'm doing."

"Keep quiet. Martin's dead."

"Jesus christ."

"Yeah. Happened the other day. Some fluke accident at rehearsal. I shouldn't have listened to his crap about not contacting me again until it was over. We wouldn't be in this mess."

"This is crazy."

"You're telling me."

"How the hell do you get killed at an opera rehearsal? Just how fucking rough an opera is it, for christ's sake?"

"I know. It's nuts."

"So what now?"

"Just go left up the hall, up the stairs and to your right. First office on the right. Put a set of these duds on. There's a guy there'll help you. Just do it and I'll explain later. And make sure the guy sees the Mossberg."

Owen Coyle hesitates, then gets to his feet, sliding the tote bag over. "Hank's been saying some weird shit," he says.

Sam nods, slides the tote bag under his chair and smiles at Harry Pazik, who grins back.

"Some game, eh?" says Harry Pazik.

"Hell of a game, Hank. Hell of a game."

Owen Coyle returns four minutes and twenty-three seconds later. Sam Labovic knows it's four minutes and twenty-three seconds later because he timed *him*, timed him like mad. Owen Coyle wears identical evening wear, the Mossberg no longer strapped to his side but bundled in what looks like a large white silk scarf.

"What the hell is that?" says Sam Labovic. "A fucking *mantilla* or something?"

"Who gives a shit? Covers the Mossberg just fine. Okay—who was that slimy bastard and what does he know?"

"Guy who works here. Doesn't know anything. Doesn't want to know anything. Caught him in the boiler room. He saw me trying to stash the bag in Marty's locker."

"How you know he won't screw us? Why's he helping at all?"

"Long story. Did you make sure he saw the Mossberg?"

"Yeah. He saw it."

"Well, that's one reason he won't screw us. We don't have much choice. We can also make a hell of a lot of trouble for him here. He's got a dope stash the size of a small drugstore down there and he's been running numbers. No big deal but he's scared shitless about it. I told him we were in a jam and pretty desperate and that made us crazy, and that my buddy, namely you, was half nuts to begin with and if anything goes wrong it's likely you'll shoot everyone in the place."

"Not far from the truth at this point."

"So, that's it. We'll get the goods out the same way Martin was supposed to. As of now, we are to the untrained eye, at least, members of the Vancouver Symphony Fucking Orchestra if anyone asks. No other ideas here."

"None here either. Do we have accents or anything?"

"Accents?"

"Yeah. Don't classical musicians all come from Europe or somewhere?"

"I do believe that some are home-grown like you and I, Mr. Coyle."

"You don't say."

"Yes, my man. I do say."

"Jesus, what a mess. What the hell happened?"

"Know anything about quantum theory?" asks Sam Labovic.

Owen Coyle (sarcastically), "Not a hell of a lot."

"Predicts probability, not the definite. Chaos, my friend, everything is random. Should read more."

"No shit."

"Instead of contemplating the vastness of space one should maybe contemplate the vastness of the minutiae, the little things. There's a whole universe as you go smaller and smaller. You know, they've even discovered an electron so small that the light needed to photograph it actually moves it aside."

"Fascinating. And all this means?"

"Details, Mr. Coyle, those fucking little things called details. It takes eighty-five individual steps to manufacture a modern golf ball. One step screws up, the whole enter-prise falls apart."

"Golf balls."

"Yes, the simple golf ball. Very complex. I screwed up,

didn't pay attention to the details. Thought I had, but hadn't. Armand and his problem, he minimized it. I should have seen it but felt it was too late to make changes. Got hasty. Or just lazy. Thought that anything that might go wrong would come from the outside, not from one of us. Forgot about the unpredictability factor within ourselves. Stupid really, and I take full responsibility."

"Fine. Here's to quantum whatever and the world of tiny things. And what about our friend here?"

Sam Labovic glances at Harry, expels a breath. "I don't know yet. Guy's obviously off his rocker and even crazier than the rest of us. We'll have to take him with us for a-ways, I guess. Be safer. Drop him off somewhere. You know something, Coyle? I don't really like having to do this to a . . ."

"Nut-case?"

"Yeah."

"Yeah. Me neither."

Mossberg "Slugster"

21

Martin Robert Sweetburne

"Labovic?"

"Sweetburne?"

And these words are exchanged innocently enough only a month and a half earlier at a chance meeting on the corner of Burrard and Georgia Streets in downtown Vancouver as Sam Labovic waits for the light, a dense drizzle glistening the streets, a chill breeze from the mountains to the north coming up off the water from the harbour.

"Long time."

"Graduation, I think."

"Heard you were doing the music thing."

"That I am."

"How's that goin'?"

"Pays the bills."

"That good, eh."

And it's then that Sam Labovic for the first time crosses the lobby of the Hyatt Regency on Burrard Street in Vancouver upon promise of a beer in the lounge to re-hash old times or maybe catch up on new ones, Martin Robert Sweetburne taking the lead to the table, planting himself, familiar with the place. Martin Robert Sweetburne of classical music leanings, of brass instruments of wide conical bore, of merino wool turtlenecks in mauve or vermillion, of Lean Cuisine frozen dinners and a fan of *faux bourdon*, a 15th century method of composition. Martin Robert Sweetburne sits comfortably at the table, furbishing details of music studies abroad after high school, of a meandering solitary life. Sam Labovic is strangely relaxed, enjoying the encounter although neither of them were ever close to the other in those much-younger days. And Martin Robert Sweetburne, a bit overweight, round face in a half-smile, savours each sip of the German beer, holding it in his mouth a moment, deliberate, patient mannerisms, much akin to those of Sam Labovic. Then Martin Robert Sweetburne swallows, the beer going down.

"So that's me. What about you?"

Sam Labovic doesn't answer.

"I've heard things over the years."

Sam Labovic takes a sip, not swallowing, beer rolling around his tongue.

"Heard you were a bank robber," says Martin Robert Sweetburne.

And there it is, easy enough, the cat finally out of the proverbial bag and Sam Labovic feeling no judgment or disapproval, and Martin Robert Sweetburne then free to ask away, questions about the lawless life and a suggestion that they continue their *parle* at his place in the West End, only six blocks to the south.

"If it was up to me I'd rather rob this place than a bank," he says as they walk back through the lobby.

*   *   *

Sam Labovic takes the two steps down into the main room, a two-bedroom, two-floor open design condominium, Martin at an ornate antiquated sideboard, pouring drinks. "Banks seem to me too risky," he's saying. "Anticipatory infrastructure throughout, ready to snare the usurpers."

Sam Labovic peruses the space, autographed headshots along one wall, bubbling aquarium, large, against another. Six red cap Orandas, some Tiger Barbs darting from a finger contacting the glass, some Gourami, and a Zebra fish motionless except for the slow wave of its tail fin just visible in a small stand of sea grass.

"And what, hypothetically speaking, of course, would that hotel have to offer?" says Sam Labovic.

Martin points a small remote at the CD player, and strange music comes out, something that Sam Labovic wouldn't know in a million years, *Tantum Ergo*, a Latin hymn from the 13th century by Saint Thomas Aquinas, a Martin Robert Sweetburne favourite. And Martin Robert Sweetburne stretches along one couch, Sam Labovic along the other. Martin Robert Sweetburne then describing two singers of the opera presently staying at the Hyatt Regency where he and Sam just were, these two stars of the theatre laden with wealth and generally believing themselves to be at one with the heavenly spheres.

"I know for a fact," says Martin Sweetburne, "that Blume himself—a painful conceit that the theatre world knows—believes in spirits, poltergeists, and the infallibility of cash. He is highly suspicious of plastic and wouldn't use a credit card to save his own life, let alone anyone else's. Hence, he always travels with a large amount of cash only, some rumours having it at a hundred thousand or more, which he would, of course, entrust to hotel security while there."

"You got to be kidding me," says Sam Labovic.

"The man's an idiot," says Martin.

"Who's the other?"

"Ah, yes," says Martin. "Then we have Ms. Fugeta, diva to the hilt, impossible to like, who, it is well-known in theatrical circles, always travels with a veritable suitcase of assorted gems and stones, with which to adorn herself at and away from the theatre. I kid you not, worth thousands and thousands."

"Jesus."

"What can I say? It's theatre. And I haven't even mentioned that the place is full for the Grey Cup. Some of those folk must have some riches, too."

More drinks are poured at the ornate antiquated sideboard, more centuries' old music, and Sam Labovic, getting ready to leave, finally examines three polished-chrome stands along another wall, three tubas of various sizes reflecting their sheen back at him. "Wow."

"Beautiful, aren't they," says Martin Robert Sweetburne. "The first modern tuba was produced in Berlin in 1835 and it's believed that French makers may have derived it by adapting valves to the ophicleide."

The ophi-fucking-what? thinks Sam Labovic.

". . . I would really like to get a B&S Perantucci PT-6 with five rotors and gold lacquer . . ."

Sam Labovic stares at the tubas. "That a tuba?" he says.

"Yes . . ."

"What's that run you?"

"Twenty thousand, Australian . . ."

"Hmm."

"And an 1891 Wunderlich and a 1922 Conn helicon I got my eye on . . ."

"Hmm."

"And a Holton H105 Double French Horn with bronze bell . . ."

"French Horn, eh?"

"Yes . . ."

"And all that . . ."

"Another seventeen, eighteen thousand."

"Will talk to you later, Martin," says Sam Labovic. "Dreams can come true . . ."

"Fortuitous running into you, Sam."

"Yeah. Same here."

22

Big Mean Surprises

JORGEN THRAPP SITS in Ron Kanavrous's office, consuming more of Ron's scotch and rethinking his meeting in the maintenance room with Sam Labovic. His hands tremble, his mind trembles. The earlier events of the day seem far off, taking on the characteristics and concocted drama of perhaps an article read in a sleazy tabloid a long time ago. And he'd like to know what power, god, or just plain ethereal bonehead, has now dumped these real-life gun-toting sociopathic prizes in his lap.

On first seeing the guy with the big gun down in the boiler room, Jorgen Thrapp freaked, assuming he was one of the undercover cops that Bernie the shit-ass had mentioned to Kenny the printer, but the guy seemed as frightened as he was. He didn't act like a cop making a bust, picking up a tote bag and forcing Jorgen Thrapp back into the maintenance room, where Jorgen nearly busted a leg tripping over a paint can. The big gun jerked at each new noise, and Thrapp made plenty of them. He watched the guy's eyes getting wider, more frenzied. The guy was no dummy, either, figuring what Thrapp was up to in a matter of seconds. The big guy's shoes scrunched over scattered pills and left footprints on the betting sheets that had fallen to the floor. Then out of the blue, he delivered an adrenalin-inspired monologue on the amount of time one can do for drug trafficking and numbers-running and didn't Jorgen Thrapp know the guy had two buddies waiting for him back in the common room? One with a sawed-off shotgun who would blow the head off a newborn baby if it looked at him the wrong way and the other an alcoholic ex-bull-rider from Little Smoky, Alberta, who may or may not be wanted for murder somewhere on the East fucking Coast and did he fucking know that, and did he want to co-operate or deal the fuck with them anyway? Jorgen Thrapp had already decided to co-operate and the guy finally stopped his rant long enough to catch his breath and gasp out his demands. Two changes of clothes, formal dress, black-tie and all that. A place to change. And a car. And did Jorgen Thrapp know where the tuba player would leave his instrument? On this last request, Jorgen Thrapp managed to find his voice. "Uh . . . I'm not sure about that, sir. Not sure if it's still in the theatre."

At this the guy stepped closer. "What do you mean still in the theatre?"

Jorgen Thrapp felt the sweat rolling down the sides of his face, and reacted to the guy's crowding by stepping to the side, his left foot wedging in a mop-wringer. The guy with the gun seemed not to notice, standing close and listening as Thrapp haltingly explained the freak accident the day before, the tuba player being laid out underneath the three-hundred-odd pounds of the director. The guy with the gun didn't say anything, just kept the muzzle level with Thrapp's midriff. Jorgen Thrapp didn't move, afraid to remove his foot from the wringer. The guy looked really nuts now. Then he backed away. Thrapp took the opportunity to pull on his trapped foot, causing more racket as a couple of mops and a broom clattered to the floor. The guy with the gun stuck it out at arm's length to within inches of Thrapp's nose, the other hand clenched at his side. *"Don't do that!"*

"Sorry."

"Jesus!"

"Sorry . . . sorry—"

"Shut the hell up!"

"Yes, sir."

"We'll have to take it out the same way with or without Martin."

"Yes, sir."

"No other way."

"No, sir."

"Of all the fucking screw-ups."

"Yes, sir."

"*Shut it!*"

"Yes—"

"You don't know what the fuck I'm talking about, do you, buddy? *So stop answering, damnit!* And you better find that tuba case, sonny boy."

And then he's allowed to leave, under heavy threats, scurrying off and pilfering two formal suits from the orchestra dressing room and finding the tuba case still in the musicians' instrument room adjoining the orchestra pit. He then gets himself back to Ron Kanavrous's office where Sam Labovic and Owen Coyle appear at one minute and thirteen-second intervals to change clothes. And he knows it's a one minute and thirteen-second interval because he timed them, timed them like mad.

He takes a long burning swallow of whisky, checking his watch. It's time. He goes to the door, opens it, and peers cautiously up and down the hall. Will he ever again leave this office without these precursory surveillances? He could call the cops, he supposes, but no, these guys are serious. The possible ramifications are too horrible to contemplate. Best to have done with it, follow instructions, and get rid of those assholes.

He lets the door close behind him, makes for the stairs down to the common room carrying the tuba case, minus the tuba as ordered, as out back, across the street from the theatre and cruising the parking lot, police officers Bean Scarfito, who is 36 years old, 6 feet, 2 inches tall and weighs 179 pounds, and Saul Jesse, who is 34 years old, 5 feet, 10 inches tall, and weighs in at 167 pounds and 3 ounces, give each other a nudge and stop their car beside a tired-looking 1990 tan Chevy Sprint hatchback with a Rent-A-Ride sticker on its windshield.

23

Dickheads and Dunces

OWEN COYLE AND SAM LABOVIC are getting more concerned (and rightly so) about Hank. The Grey Cup game has taken yet another turn for the worse for the Stampeders and Hank is writhing in his chair, unable to contain himself, with each move rendering his weird spastic dance. There's now almost a full dozen empty beer cans at his feet.

"Letting him get stupid such a good idea now, you think?" asks Owen Coyle.

"Just let him stay happy for the time being," says Sam, himself now unconvinced.

"Christ, what else can we do," says Owen Coyle. "Now I think he thinks he's an employee here, for christ's sake."

Sam Labovic checks his watch just as Jorgen Thrapp

appears, fidgeting in the doorway. Sam Labovic licks his lips, glances at Coyle. "Goofball's right on time. Let's do it."

Coyle gets to his feet. Sam Labovic turns to Harry, raising his voice so all can hear. "Come on, Hank! Your friend's parked out back. He's only got a minute to say hello, so let's make it quick!"

Harry gives him an uncomprehending look. Owen Coyle slaps him on the back good-naturedly, at the same time lifting him forcibly by the arm. "Yeah, Hank. Let's go. Won't take a minute."

Together they pull him to his feet. They feel him resist, Harry looking frantically at the TV and back at Owen Coyle. Then he casts an equally desperate look at Sam Labovic. Some of the maintenance crew turn around.

"Hey, Hank! Where you going? It's almost over. Calgary's on Toronto's thirty-yard line for christ's sake!"

Sam Labovic shrugs his shoulders, tries to smile an apology. "Just be gone a minute. He's got a friend he's got to see."

Harry Pazik is making strange sounds, pointing at the TV. One of the maintenance crew reaches under his chair and fishes out an MP3 player with headphones, tossing it to Owen Coyle.

"Give this to Hank. Got it out of Lost and Found. He can get the game on the FM tuner. Take it so he knows we're not shittin' him when he loses the point spread. Just bring it back. Ha-ha."

Owen Coyle mutters a hurried thanks, aiming Harry for the door. Sam Labovic picks up the tote bag and follows behind, giving Jorgen Thrapp a nudge in the doorway. Jorgen Thrapp opens the tuba case and Sam Labovic dumps the tote bag in, latching the case shut and carrying it himself. Once in the hallway, Owen Coyle slaps the MP3 player into Harry's hand and jams the headphones on his head, causing Harry's leg to jack-knife. Jorgen Thrapp hurries ahead of the group, deciding to keep at least a safe distance from the wacked-out poor dunce of an alcoholic ex-bull-rider in the cowboy hat just in case something goes wrong. And if something does go wrong he would prefer a clear path to hoof it, to get a lead on these guys. Harry lets go a moan with another jack-knife, as one floor above them onstage, as if in sympathy, Violetta lets go a moan too, a high octave, herself now bed-ridden with tuberculosis. "OooooOOOOOooooOoooolaaaa . . ." she sings.

*   *   *

Outside, officers Bean Scarfito and Saul Jesse walk slowly towards the Queen Elizabeth Theatre through the public parking lot across the street. Four more unmarked police cars have appeared and arranged themselves on the roadways surrounding the lot. Police on foot are fanning out toward the different buildings adjacent to the area as officers Bean

Scarfito and Saul Jesse see the bright orange fire doors of the theatre open and a tall skinny guy wearing reflector sunglasses emerge, pausing to turn and say something to someone inside the door. The skinny guy turns back, then proceeds down the steps, followed closely by a chubby guy in a western-style suit wearing a cowboy hat and clutching something with wires running to his head. At first, officer Bean Scarfito mistakes it for some kind of medical aid-thing as it appears the guy is physically handicapped in some way.

"Looks like one of those Calgary dickheads we been arresting all week at the Hyatt, Jess."

Officer Saul Jesse crouches and peers hungrily into the window of a bright red Dodge Magnum r/t. "Holy shit. Take a look at this baby. Leather seats, six-speaker sound system . . ."

Bean Scarfito stops to wait for him, turning back to watch the fire doors. Two men in formal attire have appeared following the first two, one carrying a tuba case and the other walking beside him with a large white scarf bundled under his arm.

"Fuck, that guy carrying a *mantilla* for fuck's sake?" says officer Bean Scarfito.

* * *

Sam Labovic and Owen Coyle don't notice the two cops standing near the bright red Magnum r/t in the parking lot across the street. Not until they're nearly at the bottom of the stairs, anyway.

"Jesus christ, we're screwed!" hisses Coyle.

"Keep moving—keep moving!" Sam Labovic hisses back, his stomach tightening. He stares straight ahead, willing his body not to suddenly bolt back into the theatre. And it's only then that Sam Labovic finds himself reading for the first time the inscription on the back of Harry Pazik's hat—jesus christ—who would do that to a nut-job?

They cross the street and enter the parking lot, Sam Labovic now fighting a stupid urge to whistle, maybe even start skipping just to show how nonchalant he is. He feels grossly conspicuous lugging a tuba case in his black formal-wear. As they thread their way through the cars, he can feel Owen Coyle's tension mounting beside him. He watches out of the corner of his eye the cop who is watching him, seven cars over on his left. And then there's the skinny geek Thrapp, a bundle of nerves, who by this time is tripping along some twenty-odd feet ahead of them—and Sam Labovic knows how far ahead he is because he's gauged the distance, gauged the distance like mad—and from those twenty feet ahead Jorgen Thrapp sees that Ron Kanavrous's car, the one he's going to give these psychopaths to get them out of his hair, is backed in against a three-foot high concrete retaining wall that overlooks a grassy slope that runs down to a truck lot another level down. He calls back to let the big guy with the gun and the psycho with the bigger gun know that he's going to have to pull the car ahead a bit so they can open the trunk. The guy with the big gun nods and Thrapp walks ahead, unlocking the door and climbing into the car. Harry Pazik maintains a jerky pace midway between the two parties, his hands cupped over his ears holding the headphones, his expressions and moans having less to do with his pain than his emotional interpretation of just how Willy Brisco's Stampeders are doing.

Thrapp starts the motor and spies the two policemen eyeing them from over the tops of the cars. He feels a rush of hope. Things may work out okay if these cops know their stuff, and if they're looking for suspicious characters, surely this little trio he's been strapped with will fit the necessary criteria. He pulls the car forward a few feet just as the guy with the big gun catches up and leans down to the window. "Stay there. You're driving. Give me the keys."

Jorgen Thrapp (as he will recall later and question many times with a sick feeling in his stomach) begins a protest, opening the door and trying to climb out. The psycho with the 12-gauge bundled under the scarf arrives and scoops the keys, pushing him back. "Another move like that, sonny boy, an' you're hamburger," says Owen Coyle.

The two men then move around the back of the car, as Thrapp watches the ex-bull-rider in the cowboy hat wander past the rear of the car and look out over the concrete retaining wall onto the truck lot below. The cowboy guy seems oblivious to what's happening around him, entranced by the events unfolding through the headphones.

Sam Labovic leans the tuba case against the retaining wall and Coyle opens the trunk with his free hand while keeping an eye on Thrapp still sitting in the driver's seat. "We might have to tie the trunk down," he breathes.

"Yeah, yeah," mutters Sam Labovic, growing impatient. The strain of the last hour or so is beginning to show. He hoists the tuba case off the ground.

"Where we going anyway?" asks Owen Coyle.

"Up the valley a-ways," says Sam Labovic.

"Excuse me a minute guys—" Officer Bean Scarfito, who has made his way in their direction through the parked cars, is only ten yards away. "—can I talk to you a minute?"

Sam Labovic stops moving, the tuba case held in mid-air. Owen Coyle walks four paces toward the front of the car before he stops, setting himself behind the driver's open door. Jorgen Thrapp hasn't moved since giving up the keys and sits motionless in the driver's seat just beside where Owen Coyle stands. He can hear the psycho's harried breathing. Officer Bean Scarfito has stopped moving and is standing between two parked cars in the row ahead of them. Harry Pazik is the only element of the tableau that remains in motion, shaking a fist and chanting, his eyes closed, his heart and soul, it appears, hooked into the secret world unfolding in the headphones, which he occasionally

192 • TOM OSBORNE

grabs with a free hand and squeezes tighter to his head. And it's then, in the back parking lot across the street from the Queen Elizabeth Theatre in downtown Vancouver on Grey Cup Sunday, with only minutes to go in the championship game, that Hank-Harry Pazik becomes for a moment himself again, once more the guy with a ranch-style home on the Bow River, a job with Borthwick & Brodson Realty, and a ticket on the forty-yard line. He remembers, the heavy mists of the West Coast clearing if only for the space of a moment, as Owen Coyle, who is 51 years old, 5 feet, 10 and 1/2 inches tall, and weighs 179 pounds, 3 ounces, yanks the Mossberg slide-action pump from its wrapping, points it through the open car-door window at officer Bean Scarfito, and squeezes the trigger.

Inside the Queen Elizabeth Theatre, one floor up, Alfredo is begging forgiveness of the sick Violetta, something about their beautiful home in Paris. "*Parigi, o cara,*" crows Heiner Blume.

Back outside, a resurrected Harry Pazik (albeit almost immediately lost again—*twisting of the brain structures and blood vessels*) turns back to the parking lot with both arms raised, his face an expression of mad joy untouched for the moment by any previous suffering.

"KOWALENKO DID IT! SIXTY-FIVE YARDS! ONLY A MINUTE AND A HALF LEFT!

Back inside, Violetta buys the farm, bidding farewell to Alfredo and the world singing, "*Addio del passato,*" and, as it's been put down in the program, "emits a cry of anguish and dies."

Back outside, neither Sam Labovic, Owen Coyle, Jorgen Thrapp, Officer Bean Scarfito, or Officer Saul Jesse know that Kowalenko has done it. Or Violetta has bought the farm. There is just too much happening.

At the blast from the Mossberg, Sam Labovic tosses the tuba case aside and goes for his gun. The tuba case hits Harry squarely across the midriff with a sickening sound. The air leaves his body in a hollow pathetic moan and Harry Pazik, unknowingly keeping with the timeless traditions of the theatre, emits his very own cry of anguish and leaves the stage, as he and the tuba case disappear over the three-foot concrete retaining wall. Jorgen Thrapp, upon seeing the barrel of the Mossberg at eye level and sticking through the open door window inches from his face, screams, instinctively yanking the door shut for protection. The barrel of the Mossberg, caught by the open window frame, travels around with it as Owen Coyle pulls the trigger, the blast obliterating the front windshield and a large part of the dashboard inside the car. Jorgen Thrapp screams again and falls limp across the front seat.

Officer Bean Scarfito sees none of this, opting to roll under a car when he sees the barrel of the Mossberg come up, letting go a tight little anguished cry of his own. It will only be later that he'll wish he'd handled the excitement with a little more moxie. In the distance, over the car rooftops, the head of officer Saul Jesse appears for an instant at the sound of the blast and just as quickly disappears again, more than content to remain hidden without shame until reinforcements arrive. And no one sees Sam Labovic, the Commander Colt in hand, leap the wall that Harry Pazik and the tuba case had moments earlier tumbled over.

24

Thingamajig Festival Things

You can't always get what you want
But if you try sometime
You just might find
You get what you need

—THE ROLLING STONES

THE CLEAN-UP CREW for BC Place begins to file into the stands through the various sections labelled A to Z at exactly 8:03 on Monday morning. From above they might appear to be small green (the colour of their overalls) elves or comic moles from some illustrated children's book, coming up from some cozy lair and squinting into the cold fluorescent glare of a domed sky and carrying with them their little mops and brooms and brightly coloured buckets to begin cleaning up. Everywhere, as far as their little eyes can see are candy wrappers, paper cups, crumpled programs, shreds of red, white, and green ribbons, red, white, and green badges of support, discarded and forgotten articles of clothing, crushed half-eaten hot dogs and French fries, rainbow smears of mustard, ketchup, relish and mayo along the seats and down along the floors, embedded with peanut shells, ticket stubs, chunks of hair, splashes of vomit, and countless wads of sputum.

The cleaning onslaught is preceded by a short pep talk (which everyone enjoyed if not wondered at) from the head clean-up crew honcho Big Tuck Pardue (two stints in Rockwood minimum Institution), who is 53 years old, 5 feet and 11 inches tall, and weighs 203 pounds and 4 ounces, who said to the crew at 8:01 that morning, "Look here, folks. It was only in fucking 1757 that Ben Franklin initiated America's first city street-cleaning service in Philadelphia. So it's a relatively new industry, history-wise I'm sayin'. Before that everyone just threw their trash into the streets. Hell, people as far back as the Bronze Age just lay down a new floor of clay or stones over the old one when the layer of garbage got to be too much to stand. Unfortunately, we can't do that here. Just be thankful you ain't cleanin' up after that tomato-throwin' thingamajig festival thing they have in some town in Spain every year. No, we got it pretty good here in this country, garbage-wise that is. So, you new people just startin' on the crew, you're gonna see some stuff out there you're gonna recognize and it'll disgust you but you pick it up anyway. An' there'll be stuff that's unrecognizable that will disgust you and you pick that up too. Remember the folks that put it there are just like you and me, for the most part, anyway, and it's just that when they attend big events, well, they're slobs. So, that's it. We need the money, but nobody wants the job. So let's just go out there and clean up the shit so we can all go home. Which is what we all want."

25

Disjunctive Theories

Harry Pazik doesn't know what he needs when he finally stumbles into the lobby of the Hyatt Regency Hotel at 1:15 Monday morning with a four-foot-long cord dangling from half a mangled headphone set still wedged on his left ear and carrying a tuba case. But he wants a lot.

He wants to remember. He wants to forget.

He wants to laugh. He wants to cry.

He wants the pain to go away and he doesn't care if it ever does. What he doesn't want is to be reminded of the last minute and a half of the Grey Cup game, where after Kowalenko does it—a sixty-five-yard touchdown, making the score Calgary 28, Toronto 24—Calgary stops a last-ditch Toronto drive with forty-nine seconds left, and then Calgary quarterback Sonny Joachim hands off to fullback Luis Jesus

to try and run out the clock but Jesus runs into someone—
who cares who—and coughs up the ball on the Calgary
twenty-one yard line where a guy nobody's ever heard of,
Perser Oberdatsk, or something, picks it up and runs it in for
a Toronto touchdown, making the final score Calgary 28,
Toronto 31.

And later, the loss discovered, he'll want his effing prized
western tie back.

The desk clerk (not Mike Hatskill on this shift) helps him
to a couch when he staggers in, and moves off to phone the
police after first removing the remaining piece of headphone
from Harry's left ear. This guy in the soiled and torn cowboy
garb makes the desk clerk nervous, rambling on about football games, big guns, and the unloving hearts of children who
don't care enough to even know when you've left home for a
few days. The desk clerk keeps his distance and maintains a
vigil from the safety of the front desk, tossing out the occa-
sional inquiry, like, "How you doing?" and getting no reply
from the guy on the couch, just ramblings, sighs, and grunts,
the seconds ticking by and thankfully no guests are wandering the lobby at this hour to see this. Some police at last
arrive, four officers, and they too keep a discreet distance
from the prone and babbling form ensconced on the couch.
And they're not sure if they should have their guns drawn or
not, one of them approaches closer, leans forward to ask
some questions of the victim, or, maybe, the perp. Harry
Pazik smiles up at him.

"Know what a 'spite fence' is, officer? It's a favourite turn of phrase relating to my profession, the real estate business. It's a fence erected for no other purpose than to irritate a neighbour. Isn't that a great thing, officer? Erecting a structure just to irritate someone. And, 'running with the land' is another favourite turn of phrase, although what it actually means is far less romantic and inspiring than the terminology. And I kind of wish the Stampeders were still called the Altomahs like in the thirties. You see, officer, I'm remembering. It's all coming back to me. I—"

At that moment an officer cracks open the tuba case, and the stolen contents of the hotel safe spill out onto the floor. Merrill Swann receives a call at his home to tell him that the stolen goods have been recovered and a hotel guest, one Harry Pazik from Calgary in Room 414, is a hero.

"Good work, I'll be right down," says a happy Merrill Swann, wide-awake and unable to sleep after the events of that afternoon. At that moment, back at the hotel, officers Bean Scarfito and Saul Jesse enter the lobby and make a rush for Harry Pazik, identifying him as the one who got away with the other guy by jumping over the wall in the parking lot across from the Queen Elizabeth Theatre. Another call is made, catching Merrill Swann just before he leaves home, informing him that his hotel guest, one Harry Pazik from Calgary in Room 414, is no longer a hero but a suspect and is being taken down to the police station for questioning.

"Good work," says Merrill Swann, still happy but now vengeful, assuring the police that he will attend the station as soon as possible to personally identify the 'terrorist dirt-ball.' "And I'm not surprised," he adds, "that it's one of those Calgary people."

Celia Pazik is not called at all until nearly sixteen hours later when Harry Pazik can call her himself and tell her he's a hero once again.

*   *   *

The story Harry Pazik tells Detective Sergeant Bolo Hisang, the first Malaysian Detective Sergeant of the Vancouver Police Department, is a jumble of incongruencies. But Sergeant Hisang does send out an All Points Bulletin on anyone called 'Hank' who may have been registered at the hotel during the robbery. The hotel manager who comes steaming into the station and launches into his own equally disjointed tirade, complete with his own disjunctive theories, doesn't help things. The manager is unable in any case to identify the suspect in the cowboy get-up as the man who held him up, and Sergeant Hisang takes note of the suspect's bandaged head, his torn clothes and bruised face, and decides the guy's been through enough and, with two other officers, takes him to the hospital as a precaution. There, an examination reveals the suspect has sustained two more fractured ribs and a dislocated finger in addition to his previous injuries, and is promptly attended to by a disapproving Nurse Worner, who scolds the suspect gently about leaving the hospital in the first place, while it appears to Sargeant Hisang she gives more shit to the police.

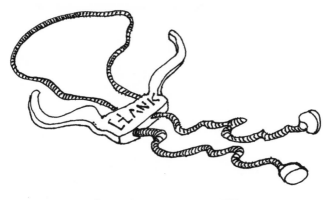

Prized Western Tie

26

No One's Safe

Sam Labovic doesn't have what he wants, which he realizes may well have been the life with the woman and the boy that somehow eluded his grasp long ago in the semi-northern logging camps of the West Coast. But he does have what he needs: about eighteen thousand in cash, plus some heavy gold bracelets and other jewellery he'd had the presence of mind to stuff in his pockets before packing the spoils from the hotel safe into the tuba case at the Queen Elizabeth Theatre. As "every handgun is a compromise for the work needed," so too is the philosophy of compromise applicable to other aspects of his life. Compromise anything, amigo, when your ass is on the line. And this last score is at least enough to get him where he wants to go, which isn't of too much importance. Maybe Miami, where in a couple of months the Super Bowl will be played. Lots of people, confusion, and capital. Or Vegas, where that's always the case. And that's the sad part, he knows, that it just doesn't matter where he goes; it's all the same, and all the wishing in the world won't change the feeling that he's never left the ships. He's still at sea, steaming full ahead, seeking landfall.

When he leapt the wall in the back parking lot across from the Queen Elizabeth Theatre and dropped onto the steep grassy slope that ran down to the truck lot below, he was sure he experienced the faint scent of some dwarf juniper, caught a glimpse of the wide green leaves and bright red berries of some devil's club and the flash of blue on brown of a ringneck snake in the tall grasses along the Nass River in northern B.C., even smelled the sharp tang of Douglas fir, bark freshly split by the choker cables as they tightened and bit, white tree flesh, the bark snapping, tree juice running. The life he maybe could have kept; the woman and the boy, it was good. The Tsimshian native kid he worked with hooking trees behind a CAT told him the eagles he saw were a good sign. Watch them, pay attention. A native's way of saying, "Get your shit together, white eyes," he hadn't figured at the time, but that was it, goddamnit, that was the message. And he rolls to the bottom of the grassy slope, ending up sprawled under one of a dozen or so semi-trailers that were parked there. On his feet instantly, he ran in a low crouch with head forward to the ground like a bloodhound on the trail. No time to worry about Coyle, or the poor nut-case Hank that he for some reason had grown almost fond of. You can't go around feeling sorry for the Hanks of the world if you want to get anywhere, and at that moment Sam Labovic wanted to get anywhere *fast*. The air was full of sirens for the second time that day as he rounded one of the trailers and spotted a woman getting into her car on the adjoining street. A wisp of cloud glowed pink across the sky above her head as the shadows lengthened. "Jesus, lady, no one's safe," he thought as he dashed forward, and grabbed the driver-side door before the woman could close it, shoved her over and levelled the big Commander Colt to a point between her eyes. And this too didn't seem fair, like forgoing the woman and the boy in the logging camps, like kidnapping the nut-case Hank, and now this poor woman, terrified and innocent, plunked by the powers of fate or whatever right into the middle of some screwball fiasco that doesn't in the least concern her. He felt again the bite of conscience as he stared at the frightened woman and put on the meanest look he could muster.

"You know what I just don't want, lady?" said Sam Labovic. "I just don't want any more fucking around."

27

Expanding Repertoires

« OWEN COYLE »

MONDAY MORNING FINDS Owen Coyle lying quietly on the cot in his cell. He needed a rest, anyway. He's tired, not just from the ball-up of the day before, but—it seems to him—from everything. From the day-to-day act of living itself, clawing his way through the years to no perceivable end, no high place where he can look around and see where he's been, how far he's come. Even how far there is to go. But he doesn't want to pull any more jobs; that's a cinch. He realizes it after the dumb shit with the reflector sunglasses yanks the car door shut just as he fires the Mossberg and blows the dashboard out through the front windshield. He only intended to fire over the cop's head anyway. Sam Labovic had disappeared, taken it on the lam he figures. Can't blame him. Cops were coming from all directions across the lot, dodging in and out of the parked cars. He watched a moment as a blue freaking heron—of all things—swooped out of nowhere and hovered on the breeze above him, as if interested in what was going on down in the world below. And Owen Coyle was a little bit interested too—you gotta take it philosophically—as he leaned up against the car and tossed the Mossberg to the pavement. That crazy bird, and himself, didn't belong there. He then pulled the Sterling .25 automatic from the holster under his left arm and tossed it over by the Mossberg. He'd been unable, as Sam earlier that morning had requested, to par himself down to "one piece apiece." Lastly, he bent down to remove the little .38 Chief's Special from his taped right ankle, contemplated using it on himself, decided against it and tossed it over with the others. And it's a real shame that he'd never been dressed better in his life and it had to end like this. He then waited quietly for the cops to move in, watching the heron drift off from its high clear place, where it can see where it's going and where it's been and although ungainly in appearance, it soared with the grace of angels, free, and in moments, was so long gone.

« ARMAND CUVALLO »

ARMAND CUVALLO, of course, has no more wants or needs, lying stone cold on a slab in the Vancouver morgue. Armand Cuvallo had never had much but he, in fact, leaves a lot. His legacy will grow with the years in the form of an expanding repertoire of conflicting stories that enlarge in extravagance from the minds and mouths of some fifteen or so Vancouver cops and twenty or so members of a certain tour group from Altoona, Pennsylvania, who witnessed his last moments while awaiting their charter bus at the front entrance of the Hyatt Regency Hotel on Burrard Street in Vancouver. He also attains fame by being featured on an episode of *Unsolved Mysteries* as a sort of "Mystery Dillinger," since no one ever claimed the body.

« JORGEN THRAPP »

A ND NOT QUITE in keeping with the perpetual preponderance of want and need, Jorgen Thrapp suffers a total collapse (which no one really needs) while lying on the front seat of Ron Kanavrous's car after the dashboard and front windshield are decimated by Owen Coyle and the Mossberg "Slugster". Thrapp is vacated, once the smoke clears, by local medics and Monday morning sees him sitting at the window in the psychiatric ward of St. Paul's Hospital, the same hospital to which the first Malaysian Detective Sergeant of the Vancouver Police Department brings Harry Pazik only hours later. And it's here that Jorgen Thrapp is able to receive, legally, all the drugs he's

212 • TOM OSBORNE

been selling *illegally* in the first place. He will stay on the ward a full month, something he wants, during which time his paranoia will drop to a mere whisper of itself, helped largely by his new friendship with officer Bean Scarfito, who believes adamantly that Jorgen Thrapp, at great risk to himself, had saved his life by bravely pulling the car door closed in the parking lot. And the Owl-man dreams too have become more friendly, the image no longer threatening but more akin to a guide of sorts, one arm pointing up, the other down, perhaps giving him choices, heaven or the gutter. He often doodles the image on scraps of paper upon which he also writes lists of exotic food orders, until he is waylaid on his twenty-eighth day on the ward by a new nurse who snatches up an Owl-man image and informs him that this image and the other earth drawings on the Nazca Plateau were actually done by extraterrestrials who visited our planet long ago . . .

Jorgen Thrapp checks himself out that very night to a new life, such as it is, as an apprentice to Ron Kanavrous in theatre lighting design. At the same time, he takes up as a hobby the late-night and early-morning laying-out in stones of his own earth drawings in local city parks and farmers' fields up the Fraser Valley, the images decipherable only from the air and sparking fear and wild speculation across the country for years to come.

The Grey Cup

28

Ovations and Citations

BERNIE THE SHIT-ASS, cop friend of Kenny the printer and not to be left out, gets what he needs six weeks after Jorgen Thrapp discharges himself from the hospital, by collaring him on a drug and numbers bust. Although the charges are later dropped due to insufficient evidence, it gives Bernie the shit-ass what he wants, which is a promotion to field detective on an undercover squad. Both officers Bean Scarfito and Saul Jesse also receive what they want in the guise of a promotion for each and decorations for (affirmed by a certified police counsellor) "abnormal bravery."

« MERRILL SWANN »

MERRILL SWANN NEEDS only that things go smoothly once again, and this he gets. He also receives a citation from the City of Vancouver and the Vancouver Police Department for "capacious bravery in the face of subversive crisis," which anyone would want. But what he doesn't need is the bill for repairs to the lobby and the rest of the hotel as a result of Grey Cup week and the subsequent police shootout with armed gunmen. The repairs and subsequent flack over expenses from the hotel owners he endures, of course, remaining ever proud of his station and maintaining a respectful aspect (on the outside at least) to the hotel guests, whatever their seemingly mundane endeavors.

On the Monday evening after Grey Cup Sunday, before going home, Merrill Swann takes the service elevator to the hotel roof where he stands awhile, looking out over the fog-misted lights of the Vancouver harbour while a biting rain and wind give him a good mauling, which he doesn't mind, and nursing a bottle of Southern Comfort while humming "Nearer My God To Thee."

« WILLY BRISCO »

CALGARY COACH Willy Brisco gets the boot from the Stampeders, which, according to Calgary is what

Calgary needs, while Stampeder quarterback Sonny Joachim, and the entire team for that matter, gets to chew out fullback Luis Jesus for fumbling the ball to lose the game. Luis Jesus, in turn, gets to blame it all on the left offensive guard, Sugar-Ray Bone, a relative newcomer who consequently is forced to bow to seniority and suffer in angry silence, waiting for his turn to tromp on the rookies next season.

« SOPHIA FUGETA »

SOPHIA FUGETA HAD already got what she needed from Jorgen Thrapp the morning leading up to opening night. That evening she received a standing ovation, which any opera star inherently wants, along with a Tuesday dinner invitation from the first black Mayor of Vancouver, which she dumps in the dressing room wastebasket on top of the flowers from Heiner Blume. (Heiner Blume himself does not attend opening night, too strung-out on the Benzedrine Jorgen Thrapp gave him, and instead spends the night pacing his hotel room, fearful not of the ghost in *Don Giovanni* but rather of the ghost of his own father, who he's convinced is clanging around in a suit of armour in the room next door, and wishes to enter Heiner's room accompanied by a theatrical mist provided by the devious special effects crew.)

« Kristy Kibsey »

Kristy Kibsey recovers herself somewhat and takes care of her needs by breaking into the tackle box of Jorgen Thrapp down in the maintenance room. She then proceeds to fall apart again by making a fool of herself on opening night, until the tackle box is nearly empty, and then she needs the next day to apologize for everything done, but no one wants any part of it.

« Mad Joe Mezzaroba »

Mad Joe Mezzaroba doesn't need anything that happens to him. The Stampeders file suit for breach of contract for his romp out on the town while on restriction (Bobby Mashtaler isn't caught) and the Canadian Football League fines him a substantial sum (exact amount undisclosed) for "unsportsmanlike conduct" during the game. He's put on waivers and forbidden to sign for any endorsements, other contracts, or even apply for a new credit card until the Calgary Club says so. In addition, his girlfriend attempts to nail him for child support (he claims the kid isn't his) and his mother weeps on the phone to him a week later from Cincinnatti, saying she can't stand all the mean things they are saying about him in the papers and the photographs with all his teeth "kicked in like that." Mad Joe remains sequestered in his luxury condominium, unavailable for comment.

29

Realms of Grace

HARRY PAZIK SINKS back on the clean white sheets and fluffed pillows of the hospital bed in St. Paul's, welcoming the attentions of Nurse Worner and moaning more with relief than pain. An unsettling memory remains of the fall over the wall at the parking lot in back of the Queen Elizabeth Theatre, and it was strange to experience the smell of bristlecone pine on the way down the grassy slope, a scent memory from fishing trips on the Bow River. And an aroma of blue spruce mingled with silver buffalo berry, some chokecherry, and hawthorn, while lying in a semi-conscious state flat on his face under a semi-trailer with a tuba case by his side. Smell (he's read somewhere) is the most predominant of the senses relating to memory. And one half of a mangled headphone is somehow still

222 • TOM OSBORNE

lodged over one ear and the audio player has pulled free and lies some feet away, but is still connected, still on, and it's during this brief period, splayed out under a semi-trailer and before blacking out again, that Harry hears the horrifying final minute and a half of play of the Grey Cup game. Consciousness will be regained an unknown time later when darkness has fallen, and he gets a waft of mountain pine this time, some potentilla, and he drags himself and the tuba case out from under the trailer. The pain means nothing anymore, there's so much of it, and his left leg now no longer even bothers to jack-knife when a spasm shoots through his body. He spies his battered white Stetson a few feet above on the grassy slope and, with help from a distant streetlight, reads for the first time the inscription scrawled in red lipstick on the back of his hat. He takes it to heart, considering all that's happened.

And now he remembers who he is. It took another bonk on the head, that's all. None other than Harry Pazik is he, seller of real estate, married with *two* kids (no dog) and the owner of a ranch-style home on the banks of the Bow River. He can even remember the last home he sold: a two-storey split-level on one and a half acres, nice, with twin carved oak doors, a rearing horse depicted on each, slate floor entrance, maple kitchen, granite countertops, ceramic rose tile floors, and vaulted ceilings with double crown moldings.

He stands—well, hunches—in the truck parking lot under the vague light from the street, and somewhere above it all, he knows, lurk the stars, twinkling down from the unrelenting vastness of space, the void of black above that stretches on, limitless, full of frightening unknowns, like the unknowns he feels stretching on in the present small void of his own life.

He clings to the tuba case as if to a rock in a stormy sea, his vision blurred, legs wobbly, but, oh, what a time it's been! Oh yeah, Harry boy. A great time, one of those great, great times. Keeps repeating this. He holds on to the deception, thinking up acceptable stories for Celia and the kids, what he can embellish to suit how he would like to remember it and have it remembered by others. And what he wouldn't give to just be having a simple iced granita at Grabbajabba in the Stock Exchange Tower back in Calgary. Or a Bow Valley Brown Ale at Brewsters on Barclay Parade, or be whooping it up with the boys at Coyotes Bar & Dance Saloon. Then in his muddled and vulnerable mind, he enters his ranch-style home, walking past the 18th century Queen-Anne-style cherry finish telephone bench in the hallway, cherry finish grandfather clock with arched bonnet pediment and reeded columns, and it really gongs too. On past the bisque-toned smooth-top electric range in the kitchen with cooktop warming zone and hot surface warning lights, Lagostina stainless steel cookware, kitchen table by the window, hideous "Patchwork Toile" patterned chair pads and tablecloth (Celia's taste), and on a rack on the wall a stainless steel ladle, pot fork, cooking spoon, perforated spoon, slotted turner, tongs, peeler, and chrome-plated whisk. Saints be praised, he remembers it all. And the hallway to the living room, where decorative ceramic plates are displayed (Celia's taste, again) and each one titled: "Farm House and Lake," "Farm House and Trees," "Farm House and Barn," "Farm House and Fields"—by god—they look beautiful. In the living room are the Victorian sofa and love seat (Celia everywhere), the wing chair by the window, everything in terrible rose floral patterns, and on the china cabinet, the twenty-seven-and-a-half inch high bronze replica of Pan, Greek god of the forest, half-man and half-goat, naked and dancing grotesquely on one hoof and blowing twin flutes. No wonder he spends so much time in the game room at the other end of the house, but what he wouldn't give to be there right now, at home that is, and sitting quietly on the rose floral patterns, not in the game room, and just, well, staring out the window on a Sunday afternoon. And he has a sudden and clear memory of his grandmother (a short three-day stint in the local lockup at Otter Rapids, Ontario, when a young girl), who was fond of referring to "The Winsome Realms of Grace," those areas of existence she felt were too often neglected and taken for granted, little gifts delivered daily by life itself, often ignored or plain unrecognized—like a child's laugh, an unexpected caress, or, yes, even just another day of breathing. Her eyes were a grassy green and with hands raised palms-out she would feign impartiality toward the listener, her message given in a voice gentle but firm: "Don't want to be preaching to you but you're never too old to make yourself smarter and cut the crap." A thought then, while hunched between semi-trailers under the vague light from the street—can head trauma actually make one wiser? And a new appreciation of what he may have in life, while at the same moment recognizing the well-lit spiral of the old Sears Tower (now Harbour something) visible over the surrounding buildings a few blocks away. A saving landmark; he isn't far from the Hyatt.

And when staring out the window of Room 414 across the bleakness of the grey downtown harbour, the tower had appeared on his right. Now it's on his left. After a few simple navigational twirls on the pavement to choose a direction, he sets off, a wiser man near the end of his journey, humbled somewhat but bearing gifts: a tuba case, an unused ticket to that year's Grey Cup, and many a raunchy tale to tell. And he leaves behind only a battered white Stetson and a prized western tie he doesn't notice.

Epilogue

MAYOR DUSTY MOONS grins into the Monday evening sports section and reads all about Mad Joe's fines and lawsuits, and Dusty Moons needs that. He then opens the City & Region section and reads about the thwarted robbery attempt at the Hyatt Regency. On the following page, he is greatly amused by an account concerning the Skirtell Women's Auxiliary, who, it's alleged, attempted to stop some Grey Cup partygoers from "performing lewd and lascivious acts" in the parking lot of their church and were consequently subjected to "all manner of verbal and simulated vulgarities." Then he folds the newspaper and pours another glass of wine, and wonders contentedly when he'll hear about his dinner date with Sophia Fugeta, which, of course, he wants very much.

JOHN THOMAS OSBORNE

AKA JT Osborne, was born on Baffin Island in
1949, and grew up in Kamloops and Vancouver.
He has illustrated various books, and is the
author of several volumes of poetry, including
Under the Shadow of Thy Wings. His first
novel *Foozlers* was published in 2004. He lives
in Maple Ridge, B.C.